Murder in the Dog Park

Bad Girl. Good Cop. Bad Dog.

by
Jill Yesko

Baxter World Publishing, Inc.
1953 Greenberry Road
Baltimore, MD 21209

http://murderinthedogpark.blogspot.com/

Editor and designer: Ruth E. Thaler-Carter, www.writerruth.com
Cover designer: Victoria Brzustowicz, www.VictoriaBCreative.com
Author photo: © 2012, Rogue Parrish, Beau Monde Press,
www.beaumonde.net

ISBN-13: 978-0-9854852-0-7

Printed in the United States of America.

To all the bad dogs at the dog park.

Acknowledgments

I would like to thank the Hampden Writer's Group for patiently listening to early drafts of the book and for complimenting me on "not writing like a girl"; Rick Shelley for editorial guidance, tea and sympathy; Ruth E. "I can write about anything!"™ E. Thaler-Carter for keeping the world safe from my mixed metaphors and for her eagle-eyed copyediting and layout skills; Linda from California for unwavering encouragement and cat-viewing via Skype; Dave for listening without judgment; Melissa Kyle of Kyle's Kennel for all things basset hound; and my brother and mother, who have always encouraged my writing.

Finally, to my pack at the dog park, thank you for your friendship and for providing me with the raw material for this novel. I promise never to bring Archie to the dog park.

1   A Body in the Weeds

I opened my eyes and saw Archie, my 90-pound black-and-white bull terrier, licking his balls at the end of my bed. Archie was a canine bad-ass with enough attitude to reach from Baltimore to Philly and then some. He'd come up on New York City's mean streets and, like most streetwise creatures, he'd quickly developed an A+ bullshit detector for sussing out dangerous situations. Archie was all rippling muscle, from his hammerhead shark-like skull to the tip of his erect, docked tail.

Archie was my doggie doppleganger. I could be a mean little bitch and, God knows, my attitude needed some major adjustment. But I didn't give enough of a damn to even try to recalibrate a moral compass. I was comfortable in my own skin, if you consider a 30-year-old woman who chases bad guys, drinks and smokes, and hacks into computers normal. And oh, yeah, I could handle a gun and studied kickboxing.

Aside from my cousin Lenny, Archie was my best friend. We'd been through more crap together than most old married couples, but, unlike my ex-husband, Archie didn't talk back or slap me around.

Archie kept me on the straight and narrow so I didn't fall down drunk or beat people up. I generally left the snarling to him. All he wanted from me was food and to run free in the dog park. I could handle that.

"Knock it off," I growled at Archie that morning, giving him a punt with my ankle. It was raining outside and I wanted to keep sleeping. I'd been up late the night before doing some deep tracking of a scumbag who'd skipped out on his wife and kids and was shacked up with another woman in Linthicum.

I liked hunting down these morons. They always thought they were so smart. Like most criminals, they severely overestimated their intelligence. I could usually locate their asses within about an hour of searching online databases. Then I sold the information to whoever was the highest bidder. What happened to these jerks after that wasn't my business

When I couldn't find them online, I'd load Archie in my battered Toyota Corolla and we'd go on surveillance missions. I liked stakeouts, even if they meant sitting in the car in the middle of the night in Baltimore's worst neighborhoods. Nobody messed with me as long as Archie was sitting in the passenger seat, snarling and baring his razor-sharp teeth.

Just in case that wasn't enough of a deterrent, I always packed an unloaded Ruger GP .357 Magnum, although I'd never had to use it. That was fine with me, since I lost my license to carry a concealed weapon after my last DWI.

Archie stopped licking his balls and walked across the bed toward me. "Don't even think about licking my face. I know where that tongue has been," I warned. Archie sat on his haunches and stared at me thoughtfully, blinking his too-small-for-his-head triangular eyes.

"Stop me if you've heard this one before," I said. "You know why dogs lick their balls? Because they can." Archie whimpered and let out a long fart—his way of telling me he didn't appreciate my joke.

I rolled out bed and pulled on a pair of jeans. The jeans fit me like a potato sack. I was already too skinny; my hip bones stuck out like barrel staves. You practically needed a microscope to locate my ass. Shopping for food was never high on my to-do list. It involved supermarkets and interactions with people. I preferred to starve.

I found a sweater and a fleece hoodie from one of the piles of clothes next to my bed. When was the last time I'd done laundry? I sniffed a pair of mismatched socks. They were stinky but would have to do. I raked my fingers through my dirty-blond hair and tried to remember the last time I'd gotten it cut. August? March?

I pulled my hair into a sloppy ponytail and cinched it with an old rubber band.

It was dark and piercingly cold as I walked bare-foot across the creaky wooden floor. I snapped Archie's harness across his muscular chest and peered out the small window next to my front door. I always checked before leaving my house. A few months back, one of the asshats I'd been tracking followed me home. I knew he was hiding in the bushes, waiting for me to leave so he could ambush me. I snuck out the back door, crept up behind him and tasered him in the kidneys. Then I opened the front door and let Archie have at him. Funny, I hadn't seen that guy since.

Shit, it was cold. I hated walking the dog in November. I hadn't had my coffee yet, so I was in a particularly cranky mood. But walking the dog was non-negotiable. Like babies, dogs could be counted on for three things: eating, pissing and shitting.

Archie pulled like a 20-mule team. I was plenty strong from kickboxing and running every day, but I was no match when Archie put himself into four-paw drive.

After 10 minutes of Archie dragging me down the road, we arrived at the dog park, a small clearing set behind a series of lacrosse fields. My shoulder ached from trying to control Archie and my toes and fingers were half-frozen.

We were alone in the park. Nobody came out at 6 a.m., which was just fine with me. I wasn't exactly a misanthrope; I just had a zero tolerance policy for idle bullshit. I cranked up my iPod whenever I saw anyone with their mutt.

"Go," I ordered, unhooking his leash. Archie bee-lined to the trees, probably after some dead rat. I trudged after him, the wet grass soaking through my Converse high-tops.

I kept my eye on Archie. He liked to take off and get into trouble. Last year, one of my neighbors found Archie sleeping on his deck after rummaging through his garbage cans. "I found your dog," the guy said, pulling up to my house in his Volvo station wagon with Archie's huge head hanging out of the window. The guy had one of those Bluetooth things around his ear.

"Everyone knows your dog is out of control," Mr. Bluetooth said. "He needs to be fixed and he doesn't have a dog license. Next time, I'm calling the cops." Archie had licked my face as I hauled him out of the Volvo and trotted behind me as I led him into the house.

"I mean it, lady. Next time, it's 911," the guy called out as I flipped him the bird and slammed the door.

People like that were way too common in my neighborhood. They thought of themselves as royalty and everyone else as their serfs. Their power-drunk ilk roamed the hallways of courtrooms and boardrooms in the downtown office towers like their shit didn't stink. Money was their common denominator. If you had money, you were golden. If you didn't have two nickels to rub together, they treated you like crap.

The rain soaked me to the bone. Archie started barking in the distance. I walked toward the edge of the field where the bare trees met the high weeds. Archie crouched and pawed the ground. The hair on his back stuck up like a hair brush. He had something in his mouth.

"Drop it, Archie!" I shouted. It was probably a dead squirrel. I grabbed Archie by his massive jowls to shake whatever he had out of his mouth. But it wasn't a turd; it was a blood-soaked sneaker.

I stood up fast, so fast the blood zoomed to my head like a coke-fueled express train. I had to squat down in the wet grass so I wouldn't puke. Archie dropped the sneaker and ran away.

It was a boy's sneaker, one of those Air-somebodies. I caught my breath and cautiously picked up the sneaker. Best to get rid of it: blood + anything = trouble.

I was about to wing it into the woods when I saw the body. The boy lay on his belly, his legs and arms at right angles to each other like a stick-man cartoon. His face was pressed into the ground. All I could see was the back of his head. Dried blood crusted over the quarter-sized wound below his left ear.

For all the time I'd spent in back alleys and drug corners of East Baltimore, I'd never come across a dead human body. I'd seen my share of road kill and even dissected a cadaver in college. Those kinds of things never bothered me. But coming face-to-face with a dead boy with a hole in his head was a new one on me. I knew I should feel something other than a deep sense that I was about to get involved in something that would complicate my life, but emotions weren't my strong suit.

I looked closer, using "soft eyes," a phrase I'd picked up from the TV show "The Wire." The boy was wearing khaki pants and a white shirt. It had to be a uniform; kids didn't dress like that if they didn't have to. His backpack lay nearby with books and papers spilling out. There was a logo on it: Park Heights Academy of Excellence. I knew that place.

I couldn't just leave the body there; I wasn't that heartless. Even for a woman who hated almost everybody, I knew a dead body deserved some respect. I called 911 on my cellphone. A bored police dispatcher told me to wait with the body until the cops came. Great. Wait by the body. Archie squatted nearby, leaving a big pile of steamy shit.

With nothing to do until Baltimore's finest arrived, I sat on a wet log and cracked my knuckles. I'd been out in the cold for almost an hour. It was getting light out and the rain had stopped. People were starting to come into the park with their dogs. I pulled my hood as far over my head as I could to ward off any potential conversation. I hoped the cops would come quickly so I could go home and drink coffee.

A Chihuahua bounded across the park and made a beeline for me. I held out my hand ready to stiff-arm the cur if he got too close. He was trailed by a blonde-haired woman in skin-tight yoga pants.

"Get the hell away from me, you mutt," I snarled as the dog closed in on me. I cranked up my iPod some more and pulled my hood even lower over my head. The woman kept walking toward me. "Jesus," I muttered. "Doesn't anyone respect personal space?"

Archie trotted over and started sniffing the dog's butt. The woman had one of those half-gallon-size Starbucks coffee cups in her hand. Her hair was perfectly styled and she had a lot of make-up on for 7 a.m.

"Is everything OK?" she said, looking down at me as I hunched lower onto the log. I had no choice but to answer. "The cops are coming. There's a dead body," I said, hoping she'd beat it.

"A dead body? The police are coming? Oh, my God, what's going on?" she screeched, pulling a pink iPhone out of her enormous handbag.

"Christ," I thought, "why can't anyone just leave things alone?" She tapped out the numbers and began leaving a hysterical message for her husband—probably some lawyer banging a younger woman. "Frank, call me right away," she shrieked. "There's a dead boy right here near the lacrosse field. Call me NOW!"

The woman bent over and stared at the child. She reached down and touched the kid's hair, like she was making sure he was dead. "I wouldn't touch the body," I said, creeped out by what she was doing. "Don't you have a yoga class to get to or something?" I said, shooting her a death stare.

I heard a rumbling sound in the distance as a dented Baltimore City police cruiser pulled up to the edge of the dog park. A tall cop emerged from the blue-and-white Crown Victoria. "Whadja got, ladies?" said the cop as he walked toward us. His dark brown hair was styled in a neat buzz cut and he looked like linebacker in a bullet-proof vest.

I eyed the Glock in his side holster as he got closer. Good-looking guys in uniforms with guns were one my few weak spots. But after my cop ex-husband landed me in the Johns Hopkins emergency room with a broken jaw, I'd sworn off men, especially men with the law on their side.

"Oh, it's just terrible, officer," wailed the woman, chewing her French-manicured fingernails. "It's a young child, a black child." She started to dissolve into sobs. "I can't believe this is happening," she went on. "It, it, could have been my son, my Jared. My God, a dead body in Mt. Jefferson ... I ..."

"It's OK, lady," said the cop, putting his well-muscled arm around her. The radio clipped to his shoulder chattered. "Sometimes Charm City isn't so charming," the cop said to no one in particular.

I knew what he meant. Mt. Jefferson was no paradise. Well, maybe for people like her—the wives of doctors, lawyers and other sushi eaters who lived in the big Victorian houses with organic gardens and Priuses in their driveways.

For the rest of us, the renters and strivers, Mt. Jefferson was just another zipcode. We knew we were the bottom-feeders in Baltimore's stratified ecosystem. Class differences still mattered here. The rich kids went to private schools while everyone else's kids were left to fend for themselves in the quagmire that was the Baltimore City public school system. That's why I didn't talk to people like her. And what were we going to talk about anyway? Lacrosse? Stock options?

"What about you?" the cop said, turning toward me. "Did you find the body?"

I couldn't lie, even though I knew telling the truth was going to drag me into a situation I wanted no part of.

"Yeah, I found him," I said with no emotion in my voice.

Murder in the Dog Park

"You're gonna have to write a statement. You can sit in the police car and do it."

The cop turned and walked toward the car. I looked at his ass. He was hot, but I couldn't get distracted by his body. I needed to protect myself from guys like him. One burned, twice shy. The cop got a yard or two before he stepped in Archie's shit. "Dammit," he said, lifting up his heavy shoe and inspecting the bottom. "Don't these people clean up after their dogs?"

I sat in the back of the police car. It smelled like pee and sweat. I scribbled fast, writing down anything I could think of so I could get the hell out of the back of the police car. I hadn't done anything wrong, so why was I sitting where they put criminals? The cop wouldn't let Archie get in the car with me. He tied him up to the door handle. Archie scratched at the window and smeared his muzzle on the glass.

I signed the statement and shoved it at the cop. "You and your dog can go," he said, smiling at me. His teeth were pearly white. "Here's my card. I'm Officer Don Williams. You can call me anytime if you think of anything else."

I grabbed the card out of his hand and untied Archie from the door handle, then slammed the door extra hard just so the cop knew how pissed off I was. As I walked out of the dog park, I turned back. The cop was busy wiping Archie's shit off his shoe.

A small crowd of dogwalkers was huddled near the body pointing and working their iPhones. Within five minutes, the pictures of the dead boy would be posted to half the Facebook pages in Mt. Jefferson.

My morning was ruined. By the annoying woman, by the good-looking cop and, most of all, by the dead boy. I tried push the images of the dead boy away but even I, a self-confessed heartless bitch, couldn't seem to do it. Why would anybody kill a kid? And why was it my misfortune to be the one to find him? I hated being responsible for anyone's problems, and death causes big problems.

My stomach growled. Coffee first. Then I'd figure out what to do about the body in the weeds.

2 Black and White and Dead All Over

Ilived in a dilapidated carriage house tucked behind a Victorian mansion. The house was worth a few million dollars and, even with the real estate market in the toilet, the place was still out of reach for anyone who didn't have Esq., MD or CEO after their last name.

I'd been renting the place since my divorce from my abusive ex. The rental agent said it was charming and cozy, which was realtor code for a dirty dump. The place was barely 500 square feet with a leaky roof, rotting plank floors and a barely functioning furnace that kept me chilled to the bone well into the hottest months. The owners of the mansion charged me a fortune, but I needed a place that was private— away from the prying eyes of my idiot neighbors and safe enough that I could come and go without constantly looking over my shoulder.

People, for the most part, annoyed the hell out of me. I was just fine living my life with Archie and my laptop. I couldn't understand why people needed to constantly be in the company of other people. Crowds gave me the jitters. Maybe I was missing some kind of social chip. Even if I was a slightly paranoid, misanthropic bitch, I had no interest in doing anything to change it.

No one could see the carriage house from the road. Even the main road itself was easy to miss. Mt. Jefferson was full of hidden lanes guarded by huge oak trees and overgrown hedges. The mansion's owners—a fat hedge fund manager and his 24-year-old Brazilian wife—were often away for months at one of their other homes around the world. During their absences, I routinely picked the locks and wandered around their house.

I wasn't going to steal anything; I just needed to see first-hand how the other half lived. If the hedge fund manager's bank and brokerage statements were any indication, I'd say the other half was kicking my ass.

For kicks, I hacked into his desktop computer and copied a few of the dozens of emails he sent to Ukrainian woman at www.hotsovietbabes.xxx. I figured I could use them as a bargaining chip next time to guy tried to raise my rent. Then I gleefully changed all of his passwords (not too smart to keep them all in a Word document labeled "P.words") just to mess with him.

After my computer escapades, I would stretch on their leather couch and drink their 40-year-old Glennfiddich while thumbing through first editions of Arthur Conan Doyle and H.L. Mencken. During the winter, I took long soaks in their indoor Jacuzzi and wore their plush terrycloth robes. I built fires in the huge stone hearth and Archie and I would fall asleep next to the glowing embers.

I could get used to this kind of life, I would think. If only I could figure out how to keep Mr. Hedge Fund and the missus on permanent vacation, I'd be set for life.

From my corner window, I could easily see around the mansion to the main road. I installed motion sensors and cameras on the inside and outside of the house to make sure I wasn't followed.

The only person who knew where I lived was my cousin Lenny, and he only stopped by when he needed money or a shoulder to cry on.

Archie jumped onto the couch and started shaking the water off his coat. A spray of muddy water stained my already-grimy walls. I sat down on my threadbare recliner and started chewing my nails. Then I got up and made some coffee. Looking out the greasy window, I saw a silver SUV approach the stop sign in front of the mansion. The car barreled through the intersection.

Asshole, I muttered. I had just enough time to catch a glimpse of the teenager behind the wheel and make out the "I Love Lacrosse" bumper sticker before the car zoomed down the steep hill to Mt. Jefferson Village.

I hated lacrosse. It seemed like every kid and his cousin in Mt. Jefferson played that idiotic sport. Every weekend, hundreds of kids and their obnoxious parents descended on Mt. Jefferson Park for lacrosse tournaments. Their monstrous SUVs blocked the narrow roads like herds of steel water buffalos. They swarmed into the park with coolers, deck chairs, and fat, slobbering Labrador Retrievers. I couldn't walk Archie in the park because the lacrosse players held games from early morning until well after dark. On Monday mornings, the fields were always littered with half-full Gatorade bottles, soggy pizza boxes, beer cans and shriveled condoms.

Archie let out a long fart and re-adjusted himself on the couch. He lay on his back with his misshapen head lolling to one side, his eyes rolled back in his head. The doorbell rang three times. Archie jerked awake and ran toward the door, barking and snarling. Three rings signaled Lenny's arrival. I grabbed my cold coffee and let him in. Archie sniffed Lenny's ass and hopped back on the couch.

Lenny was a piece of work. He was short and fat—the sloppy kind of fat that even expensive clothes can't hide. Not that Lenny would even try to dress up. He wore his usual outfit—a stained red flannel shirt, brown polyester pants and black Reeboks with holes in the toes. The logo on the dark green baseball cap tamping down his shaggy hair read

"Rock Star"—the irony of the phrase no doubt lost to Lenny. As usual, he smelled as bad as he looked, somewhere between dog breath, old corn nuts and eczema cream.

Without asking, he shuffled in, settled his bulk on the recliner and started fiddling with one of the ancient 35 mm cameras that always hung from his blotchy neck on a worn leather strap.

I had to say something; he could sit there all day doing and saying nothing, just making me antsy. "What are you shooting today, Lenny—drowned rats?"

"Oh, that's funny, Jane."

I wasn't sure he got the joke.

"What brings to you my humble abode?" I said, putting a cup of coffee in his outstretched hand.

"I brought you a 30th-birthday gift," Lenny said. "I thought you might like to celebrate in style." He rummaged through his ancient backpack and pulled out a wine bottle.

"What is that swill?"

"A rare 2009 Bosquet des Papiers Chante Les Merle," Lenny said proudly. "It's a 'full-bodied red from the Rhone Valley with spiced jam and plum notes and an herbal aroma.' It retails for $100 a bottle."

"You sound like that idiot from 'Cellar Notes,'" I snorted. "Where the hell did you get something like that? Were you dumpster-diving behind Wells Liquors again?"

"I am deeply offended by that remark," Lenny said in mock horror. "If you must know, I found your gift behind the Wilson house on Greenspring Avenue after their daughter's wedding. They were throwing out cases of half-empty liquor bottles and uneaten food. I've got a whole freezer full of beef bourguignon and a quarter of a wedding cake that should keep until summer."

I took a closer look at the bottle while Lenny pulled a rawhide out of his back pocket and tossed it to Archie. The two of them were thick as thieves. They had a lot in common: They both smelled awful and didn't mind eating out the garbage.

I held the bottle up to the light and tried to translate the label with as much success as my ninth-grade French would allow. The bottle did look expensive. How long had it been since I'd even had a glass of wine, much less a good one? Or a meal that didn't come from a pizza box? After all of the Natty Boh and Bud Ice I'd been drinking the last three years, I wasn't sure my system could handle alcoholic beverages that cost more than a minimum-wage working grunt could afford.

Lenny knew wine. He used to have a wine cellar and talked about going on a wine-tasting tour to Italy when he retired. Even though he looked like a

18   *Murder in the Dog Park*

bum, back in the day, Lenny was a star photographer for Baltimore's morning and evening newspapers. It was the rare day when his shots weren't featured on the front page. People compared Lenny's photography to Weegee and Aubrey Bodine. For a decade, Lenny was always off on assignments to Annapolis, shooting the governor or visiting dignitaries. For a few years, he was a regular at the National Press Club in DC. He even took some pictures for National Geographic.

Things started going wrong for Lenny about the same time the newspapers started folding. The photographers were the first to be laid off, followed by reporters and copyeditors. Lenny's wife left him when the money ran out and he had to sell their rambling house near Mt. Jefferson Park. Lenny moved into a dingy Section 8 apartment in Upper Park Heights. In short order, he gained 75 pounds, crossed bathing off his to-do list and stopped going out in the daytime. The one thing he didn't give up was photography. He set up a darkroom in the corner of his already-dark apartment. Every inch of wall space was covered with black-and-white pictures of Mt. Jefferson. I knew Lenny creeped most people out, but I also knew he was OK. We had been as much best friends as cousins for most of our lives.

The last few years had been tough for Lenny. With no work, he spent his nights roaming the streets and alleys of Mt. Jefferson, taking pictures of trees, cars, rocks, birds and children. He had been picked up by the cops a few times and told to knock it off, but he kept doing it. I knew he was harmless, but try convincing the mommy brigade of his innocence. In their eyes, he was just a notch under John Wayne Gacy.

One day, while I was walking Archie I found Lenny, breathing like a steam train, crouched behind the dumpster next to the local elementary school.

"What the hell are you doing, Lenny?"

"They were going to kill me," he panted. "I just wanted to take some shots of the kids playing at recess and the next thing you know, the security guard and the teachers are grabbing my cameras and chasing me. I don't understand what's wrong with them. Why would they treat me like an animal?"

That was awhile ago. Now here he was in my living room, obviously worried about something. "You want some more coffee, Lenny?"

"Not now. I need to show you something."

His right leg began jackhammering up and down, a sure sign that he was about to deliver bad news.

He reached into his backpack and pulled out some black-and-white prints. "I shot these last week after the big lacrosse tournament at Mt. Jefferson Park," he said, tossing a sheaf of pictures onto my lap.

I thumbed through pictures of well-muscled teenage boys holding their lacrosse sticks aloft, their bodies twisting into ecstatic contortions, every muscle deeply accentuated. Lenny captured their youth and focused exuberance in a way that made me gasp. As much as I hated lacrosse, the boys in the pictures looked pretty hot. Lenny really did have a great photographic eye.

He had singled out one particular player who was taller and more well-built than the rest. Picture after picture showed this terrifying gladiator sprinting up and down the muddy field, gripping his lacrosse stick like a medieval mace, smacking his exoskeleton-like frame into the other kids before launching the hard, white ball into the net with so much force I could almost hear the net rip. His bicep and thigh muscles looked like they owed a big debt to steroids. A demonic glint flickered in his eyes. I didn't know characters like this existed outside of video games.

"Who the hell is this Aryan abomination?" I asked.

"That's Jared Legg-Alexander," said Lenny. "He once beat the shit out of me, and I didn't even have my camera that day. I think he did it just to be an asshole."

I started flipping through the rest of the pictures. Lenny had followed Jared into the parking lot after the game. There were shots of Jared, sweaty and stripped to the waist, fist-bumping and man-hugging his buddies. They all had cans of beer in their hands. In another picture, a blonde woman with what looked like fake boobs hugged Jared.

"I know this woman!" I said. "She's the crying bitch from the dog park who was there when I found the body of that kid. She cried a river and acted really strange around the body. She probably had to take the rest of the day off and get a spa treatment to deal with it."

"She's the brute's mother," Lenny said. "They live in the really big house at the top of West Bend Drive. Old family money there. Lots of it."

"Well, fuck me royal, Lenny. Sounds like our kinda folks," I said with acid in my voice. "But Ms. Moneybags and her son the Incredible Hulk can both kiss my ass."

"I hear they have a yacht in Annapolis and a home in Aspen," said Lenny.

The more Lenny told me about these people, the more pissed off I got. I needed a drink and a few hours on the heavy bag to work off my anger.

Lenny lifted his saggy butt out of the recliner. He put his coffee mug on the floor so Archie could finish it.

"Thanks for the coffee. I gotta catch the bus down to the VA to get my diabetes meds."

I slipped a fiver into Lenny's clammy hand.

Murder in the Dog Park

"For an Egg McMuffin, Lenny. You deserve a break today."

He laughed. This time I'm sure he understood it was a joke.

"Thanks again. You're my only friend."

Oh, crap. I hated when he got all sentimental on me. "Get the hell outta here, Lenny, before I de-louse you." He half-smiled as he reached for the door. As he turned the door knob. I noticed a wet spot on the rear of his pants. I was going to have to use half a can of Lysol to get the smell out of my recliner.

"See you tomorrow," Lenny called out. "Tomorrow I'll bring some new pictures. I think you're really going to be interested in them."

And then he was gone.

Murder in the Dog Park

3 Not a Kodak Moment

My mother loathed Lenny from the first time she laid eyes on him. "That boy is not right," she declared, giving him the stink eye. "He looks like my uncle Janucz, the village idiot."

Lenny and I grew up together in Mt. Jefferson. His parents—my father's brother and his wife—immigrated to the United States a few years after our family. Lenny's parents never learned English and Lenny spoke with a Polish accent until junior high school, much to the embarrassment of my mother.

I never asked my mother what she had against Lenny. After my father died, I realized it wasn't Lenny who got under her skin. I think my mother was annoyed at my father for sponsoring his brother and family when we were barely making ends meet ourselves. Our rent was always late and neither of my parents had steady work, even though they had college degrees.

Lenny's parents were what my mother called "potato peasants"—an insult she reserved for anyone who didn't come from Warsaw. They smelled like sausages and had little interest in assimilating into their new lives as Americans. Tadeusz, Lenny's father, sat up all night drinking vodka and weeping. "Stop crying about the old country," my mother would scold him. "You're in America now. Get a job and sober up."

My father must have been sending money to Poland for years before Lenny and his freeloading parents arrived on our doorstep. Little did Lenny and his family realize that my parents had lost everything they owned to come to the United States. We weren't the rich American relatives they thought we were, and life in America wasn't the fantasy they'd constructed from behind the Iron Curtain by piecing together snippets from illicit Voice of America radio broadcasts and letters smuggled in from distant relatives who'd settled in Milwaukee.

"The Communists took everything from us that wasn't nailed down," my mother lamented to me on a weekly basis. "And what they didn't take, your father's family did." She hated that Lenny's parents refused to change their last name—Valcheck, our original last name, was never mentioned. Before they left Poland, my parents had already selected Ronson as their new American last name. I think Mom found it in one of the contraband British newspapers that would sometimes mysteriously appear on our dining room table.

"Who in America can pronounce Pryzgyocki?" my mother would say.

My mother never gave in to Lenny's parents with any grace. "Maybe if you learned English and changed your last name to Kennedy you could get a job," she said to Lenny's father accusingly one night, after he'd asked her for $100 to buy a TV. "Then you wouldn't be in my kitchen every week like a dog begging for a bone. And your son doesn't look like he needs any more of my gwumpke. He's fat enough."

Lenny's parents eventually found jobs working double shifts inspecting hot dogs at the Esskay factory in East Baltimore. Since they were never around, Lenny became our responsibility. I felt bad for him; he may not have been the sharpest tool in the shed, but he was my only cousin and my only friend.

Lenny spent every afternoon at our apartment. After eating double portions of my mother's dumplings, he usually fell asleep with his mouth open on our ancient couch. As a playmate, Lenny wasn't much fun. He was fat and uncoordinated. The other kids in the apartment building taunted him because of his accent and tendency to fart and hiccup at the same time. He wasn't much of a student, either. His grades usually hovered in the C to C- range. I hated when his parents compared him to me—something they took sadistic pleasure in doing.

But what Lenny lacked in social skills, he made up for in his aptitude for photography. One day, he came home with a broken Olympus OM-1 35 mm camera that he'd filched from a neighbor's garbage can. He spent the next week hunched over our coffee table, painstakingly disassembling it. I watched as Lenny dripped sweat over my mother's hand-crocheted doilies, his chubby hands turning the camera over as he examined the shutter. "Aha," he said triumphantly. "The problem is the negative meniscus and a jammed Cassler mechanism. I can fix this."

Within a week, Lenny was hitting me up for money so he could buy film for his newly fixed camera. Since I didn't have any money, we decided to shoplift the film from the downtown camera store. I knew stealing was wrong, but we were broke and too young to get jobs. This caper was going to our secret.

Lenny insisted on wearing the camera around his neck while we walked the three miles to the camera store. We could have taken the bus but we decided to save our pennies for candy and sodas. The camera bounced against Lenny's breastbone with his every flat-footed step.

As we walked, we hatched a plan: Lenny would ask the salesman to put several rolls of film on the counter while I asked to use the bathroom. Then Lenny would pretend to sneeze and knock the film off the counter onto the floor. Before the salesman could make his way around the counter to pick up the film, I would run over, scoop all the film canisters

Murder in the Dog Park

and run out the door with Lenny right behind me. The plan seemed foolproof.

Lenny huffed and puffed as we walked along Charles Street, smelling the exhaust of the cars heading home from downtown. We passed the Washington Monument and stopped in front of the Walters Art Museum. "My mom says they have suits of armor and all kinds of cool stuff about knights in there," said Lenny.

Neither one of us had ever been to a museum. The public school we attended in Baltimore barely had enough money for books, let alone field trips, but somehow Lenny had gotten hold of a catalogue from the Walters with pictures of medieval armor. He kept it under his bed with his Spiderman comic books.

"We've got no time for museums, and why do you care so much about knights in shining armor?" I hissed. "It's not like King Arthur ever lived in Baltimore."

Lenny ignored me. He sat down on a bench in the park across from the Peabody Conservatory and munched some M&Ms. When those were done, he pulled some dusty Necco Wafers out of his pocket and put them in his mouth two at a time.

"At this rate, the camera store is going to be closed by the time we get there. And we're going to have to walk home in the dark. Move it!" I ordered.

"This is as fast as I can go. My feet hurt," Lenny whined.

"It's not your feet that are the problem, it's your stomach. Why are you always eating all of our food? Don't your parents feed you?"

"I don't like their food. Your mom is a better cook. My parents are always yelling at me for being too fat. I can't help it if I'm always hungry."

I grabbed the last few Necco Wafers out of Lenny's hand and threw them into the street.

"Do you want to steal that camera film or not?" I said crossly.

"Sheesh, Jane," Lenny pouted. "I just wanted to admire that scenery for a little bit. We never get to this part of town."

We arrived at the camera store five minutes before closing. The shop was at the end of a long row of old storefronts at the end of the downtown strip, near the old trolley tracks. I recognized a few of the stores: DePasquale's Bakery, Kelly's Beer and Liquors, and the abandoned stationery store still stocked with old greeting cards, wrapping paper and faded paperback books.

I'd only been to the camera store once before and had forgotten that the owner used a buzzer to let customers in the locked door. In the thin winter light, the cameras in the window reminded me of one-eyed robots.

I felt scared and thought about heading home. But we'd come this far and I didn't want Lenny to know I was losing my nerve.

Lenny rang the buzzer. It sounded sharply. I walked in behind Lenny with my head tucked into my neck. Lenny ambled up to the cracked glass counter stocked with rows of cameras.

"Can I help you?" asked the salesman, his back to us. He was bent over an old wooden worktable, fiddling with a dissected camera. "This had better be quick, it's almost six and I don't stay late for nobody."

"I want to see the new Leica M5," said Lenny. "And I need some film." The man slowly turned from his table and looked at Lenny.

"What kinda film you want, kid?"

"Kodak ASA 400," said Lenny with more confidence than I'd ever heard in his voice. "But I want to see that new Leica first."

Damn it, Lenny. You need to stick to the plan. Forget about the camera and just get the film. I stood behind him and kicked his heel. "Oh," he said. "Can I also get five rolls each of 100, 200 and 800 Ektachrome."

I hid behind Lenny's bulk. The man bent down and extracted a camera from the showcase. He gently placed it on a worn velvet square for Lenny to inspect.

"This here's the top-of-the-line Leica. Just got it in from Japan last week. What's a kid like you gonna do with a camera like this?" he asked, staring right at Lenny. "I'm guessing you don't have any money. You some kind of looky-lou? I don't have time for that kind of rubbernecking in my store."

Lenny started to slump. I kicked his heel again, harder this time. "OK, maybe I'll just take the film," said Lenny.

"You sure you got the money for all this?" the man said, looking Lenny up and down, then peering over his shoulder. "That your little sister behind you?"

"Yes, it's my little sister. She's very shy," said Lenny. "May I have my film, please." The man turned and started pulling yellow-and-black film canisters from a high shelf behind the counter. "Hurry up, Lenny," I whispered in his ear. "My mom's going to kill me if we get home after seven. And I'm going to kill you if I get in trouble."

I crouched lower behind Lenny. I needed him to get this over with quickly. We were already in uncharted territory and I had a bad feeling that Lenny was going to screw up.

The man put the film on the counter. Lenny picked up the canisters one by one and held them up to his thick glasses. "They're all genuine Kodak film, made in the US of A, son," the man said, adjusting his thick glasses. "That's going to be $35 plus tax for all them rolls. Hope you got enough cash on you 'cause I know you're too young to have a checking account."

This was my cue. "I need to use your bathroom. It's an emergency," I said, stepping out from behind Lenny.

"I don't have a bathroom for little girls here," the man said. "You need to ask over at DePasquale's, but they're all probably closed up by now."

I hadn't figured this would be a problem. "It's OK, I can use a men's room," I said, stalling for time.

"Like I said, no bathroom for girls here. You're just gonna have to hold it in. Now pay up and get out. It's way past closing time and I'm late for my bowling league 'cause of you two."

Achooo! I fake-sneezed, hoping Lenny would take his cue. *Achoo. Achoo.*

"Tarnation, girl, I don't want your snot all over my expensive merchandise. Both of you, get out of here now!"

I elbowed Lenny in the ribs. *Achoo*, he sneezed, placing his sweaty hands on the glass display case. *Achoo. Achoo. Achoo.* While Lenny was sneezing, I quickly unzipped my backpack and started sweeping the film into it. Lenny was too deeply involved in sneezing to notice what was going on. With each sneeze, his body lurched forward. I reached my skinny arm around Lenny and managed to get most of the film in the backpack before the salesman could react.

"Let's go!" I shouted.

But Lenny kept sneezing. It was too late. The man grabbed Lenny's arm. "I knew you two were up to no good! I'm calling the cops."

Should I cut and run, or stay with Lenny and face the humiliation of going to the police station, followed by the embarrassment of having my mother come get us?

I ran.

I sprinted toward the door and yanked it open. The cold night air hit me in the solar plexus like a fighter's upper cut. I ran down the now-dark street toward Lexington Market. I ran past homeless men in torn overcoats. "Slow down, little girl, what's your hurry?" one called out after me. I pulled open the market's heavy door and stopped by a butcher's stall to get my bearings. My heart had never beaten so fast. At least I had the film. But what good was that going to do if Lenny couldn't use it? I didn't need film. This was all supposed to be for Lenny. I hadn't really thought this plan through. Everything was going all wrong. Lenny's parents would probably take his camera away and ground him for a few weeks. My mother would ground me too, along with applying a few well-placed swats to my butt with a wooden spoon.

"You need something?" the butcher in a blood-stained apron asked as I stared at a dozen pigs' feet on a bed of ice chips. "I got some sausages on sale you can bring home to your mama." I glanced at the blood-red chops and whole chickens in the butcher's showcase. I felt like I was going to throw up.

Outside the market, I squatted down with my back against the building's rough brick wall. I'd screwed up. But so had Lenny. If he hadn't diddled around so long with that camera, we would have been out of there and halfway home by now with a knapsack full of film and no one the wiser.

I couldn't stop feeling bad. I'd left Lenny in the lurch. As much of a pain in the ass as he was, he was the closest thing to a brother I had. Like a bad penny, I knew he would keep coming back. We were stuck with each other, for better or for worse. But what could be done to fix the situation? Deep down, I knew what I had to do to make this right.

I slunk back to the camera store. All the lights were off. Lenny and the salesman stood by the door, waiting for the cops to arrive, I paused, sucked in my gut, squared my shoulders and rapped on the door. The sound of the buzzer shot through me. I walked into the store and tossed my knapsack on the counter. "Here, mister. Take all of your film back," I said, mustering up as much authority as a 4'10" 12-year-old-girl could. "Now please give me back my cousin."

Lenny looked worse than the time the principal called him an imbecile during a parent-teacher conference. His eyes were red and his nose was wet. I was sure he'd been crying non-stop since I took off. "You think you can just march on back in here and I'll forget about this?" the man chuffed. "The cops are coming. You two are going to wait here with me."

The man unzipped the knapsack and started restocking the film. I was boiling mad. I contemplated hurling the knapsack at the back of his head. Why wouldn't this guy just let us go? Why did this grey-haired idiot want to make an example of two kids?

"Mister," I began, "I returned the film ..."

There was a rap on the door. A cop's profile appeared, silhouetted against the frosted glass. When the buzzer sounded to let him in, Lenny started sobbing.

"What's the fuss about, Bill?" he said, tamping his hat on and yawning.

"Got myself two little shoplifters right here. Caught them both red-handed, trying to steal me blind."

"They don't look like trouble to me. What'd they take?"

"The fat one tried to steal one of my new Leicas and the little girlie made off with a bag full of film."

The cop looked at the empty backpack on the counter. "Where's the film?"

Murder in the Dog Park

"It's all been re-stocked," the man said. "And the Leica's locked in the rear safe."

"Then you ain't got much to worry about," the cop said, looking at Lenny who was blubbering into this sleeve. "I'd say you should let these two go. Must be way past their supper time. Bet their mama is worried."

I'd never met a cop before. My mother told us to stay away from the police and mind our own business. But this cop seemed OK. He was short, with his gut bulging over his blue serge uniform and hanks of yellow-white hair sticking out from under his hat.

The camera-store owner seemed to be trying to figure out how to get rid of us without looking bad in front of the cop.

"Tell you what, Bill. Why don't I run these two home and then we'll ride over to Burke's for a few cold ones?"

The man squinted at me. He looked me up and down and spat. I knew he knew I was the mastermind behind this affair.

"If I ever see either one of you again, I won't be so charitable," he scolded. "You're damn lucky that Officer Moynahan has a soft spot for little Pollacks like you. If it was up to me, you two would be on your way to juvie hall by now."

I could feel the rage rising in me again. I gritted my teeth and balled up my fists. I wanted to clobber this guy, break all the glass cabinets and throw his stupid cameras into the street. Instead I directed my anger at the easy target—Lenny.

"I hate you," I screamed at him. "Stop crying like a big baby and grow up, you fat turd."

Lenny just kept sobbing. This was not a Kodak moment. I knew I'd hurt him bad. We were off the hook, but I didn't feel any better for it. I'd been humiliated and, worse than that, for no reason—we'd failed in our mission. Now we were heading home empty-handed in the back of a police car.

I vowed that I'd never find myself feeling this helpless ever again. Next time, I'd fight back with everything I had. I'd defend Lenny or myself, no matter what the consequences, and we would win.

4 Murder Frame-by-Frame

The clock read 1:30 p.m.—time for a beer. I opened the refrigerator and reached for a can of Natty Boh. I probably should have eaten something first to stave off an alcohol-induced migraine, but the only thing in the refrigerator was a two-week-old half-eaten pizza. It would have to be a liquid lunch again.

I cracked open the beer and grabbed the stack of pictures Lenny had left on my dining room table. I took a long gulp and belched. I settled onto the coach with Archie to let the alcohol take effect. The alcohol hit me like a fastball to the gut and, by the time I downed the can, I had a good buzz going. After my second beer, I began looking at the pictures.

My attention was riveted to the first picture Lenny took of Jarred Legg-Alexander. The kid was stripped to the waist and held his lacrosse stick aloft like Thor hoisting his deadly hammer. Yeah, that Jared kid sure looked good half-naked, never mind that he was a good 20 years younger than me. What the hell, I thought, a girl can dream. I'd flipped through about half of the pictures when something else caught my eye. In the far corner of the picture of Jared and his buddies taking practice shots at the lacrosse goal, I saw a familiar figure. I took another swig of beer and gasped.

Jesus, it was the dead kid from the dog park. Only he wasn't dead. He was sitting cross-legged at the far edge of the field, not 10 yards from where I found him. His elbows were pressed against his knees and his hands cupped his face. He was staring intently at the lacrosse players with a look of wonder in his eyes. Lenny must have been patrolling the perimeter of the lacrosse field to have gotten that shot.

In the next picture, Jared Legg-Alexander's head was turned toward the boy. I couldn't see Jared's face, but his body language wasn't friendly. I rifled through the rest of the pictures. The sequence showed it all in rapid succession, like an old-fash-ioned movie flipbook: Jared scooping up a ball with his lacrosse stick. Jared raising the stick over his head. Jared launching the ball toward the boy. Boom, boom, boom. The boy falling down. The boy disap-pearing from the picture. Jared turning toward the camera. Jared grinning like a sick maniac.

I got up and puked. I wanted to believe it was too much beer on an empty stomach, but I knew it was from having seen a boy murdered frame-by-frame. Jared Legg-Alexander killed the boy and left him to rot in the dog park with a bloody hole in the back of his head. I drew in my breath, then exhaled force-fully.

Shit, Lenny. You saw the whole thing—and now you've dumped it in my lap to sort it out. I grabbed my cellphone and punched Lenny's number into the aging Nokia. "Lenny, get your ass over to the lacrosse field *now*," I screamed into his voice mail. I wasn't drunk anymore. I was livid. "Archie, here!" I ordered. Archie hopped off the couch. I put his harness on and headed out to the dog park. "It's ass-kicking time, Archie," I said as he picked up the pace. "Jared Legg-Alexander is a dead man."

Lenny was at the lacrosse field by the time Archie and I jogged over.

"You'd better not lie to me," I said, standing nose-to-nose with him and jabbing my index finger into his well-padded breastbone. "What the hell went down on that lacrosse field?"

"I was scared to tell you," Lenny said, unable to meet my gaze. "I was out shooting the lacrosse games and I saw that little kid. He was watching me photograph those lacrosse boys. I saw that lacrosse monster kill that poor little boy. But who's going to believe me? Everyone in Mt. Jefferson thinks I'm Boo Radley."

"But what the hell, Lenny, you photograph a murder and then show me the evidence! Ever heard of going to the police?"

"I can't go to the police. They'll lock me up again, like last time."

A year ago, a cop arrested Lenny for taking pictures of kids drinking six-dollar triple frappuccinos outside of Starbucks on Roland Avenue and charged him with trespassing and suspicion of being a peeping tom. I bailed Lenny out of the city jail. I warned Lenny to cut that crap out and leave people alone, but he insisted he needed some pictures of people kissing for one of his portfolios. Springing Lenny from jail set me back $500 I was never going to see again. And he didn't even thank me.

"You'd better start talking and start talking fast," I growled. "From the beginning, what happened?"

"It's like I told you—that boy was sitting there at the edge of the field. Jared saw me taking pictures and I panicked. So I starting taking pictures of him so I wouldn't have to look directly at him. You know I get embarrassed when people look at me."

"Yeah, yeah," I hissed. I was in no mood to hear about Lenny's neurosis du jour. "And then what?"

"Jared Legg-Alexander saw the kid watching him and shouted at him to beat it. But the kid wouldn't leave. He was, I dunno, kind of transfixed. So Jared starts scooping up lacrosse balls and whaling them into the net.

"The next thing I know, he hurls a ball at that poor kid's head and the kid just drops like a damn stone. I put my camera away and started running. I was sure Jared was going to kill me next."

"Oh, God, Lenny. You coward," I started to say. "You should ..."

"Wait, I'm not done," Lenny said, ratcheting up his voice. "Stuff happened after that. And it's worse."

"What could be worse than watching a kid get murdered by a savage teenage mutant and keeping your damn mouth shut about it?"

Lenny's face turned white. He could barely get the words out. "Jared Legg-Alexander and his mother are going around saying I killed the kid. You know how everyone hates me. They're going to try to pin this murder on me. I already heard them talking about it with that lawyer husband of hers. I was eavesdropping on them under their window last night. They're going to the police tomorrow. I'm getting framed."

I felt something poke me in the butt. I turned to see Archie's cone of a nose in my ass. I unleashed him and watched as he loped over to a tree and peed. Archie had better not find any more dead bodies, I thought as I turned back to Lenny.

"Look Lenny, you've got nothing to worry about. We've got the photographs showing that Legg-Alexander psycho murdering that kid." I said.

"This whole thing is a big mistake, and we're going to fix it."

"I hope so, Jane, or else I'm going to spend the rest of my life in jail," Lenny said with solemn conviction. "My miserable life will be over."

"Don't be such a drama queen. You'd better stay in that black hole of an apartment of yours until this all dies down," I said sternly. "These people can do some serious damage. You lie low until I tell you it's OK to pull your head out of your ass. Got it?"

"OK," Lenny said obediently. "Can I have some money for bus fare?"

For the second time in a week, I shoved a five-dollar bill into Lenny's sweaty palm.

He gave me a sheepish nod and walked away.

Yeah, Lenny was in a fine mess, and once again, it was my responsibility to be on clean up duty.

"Shit," I said to Archie. "Lenny's screwed."

5 Monday Night at the Hub Cap

I started pacing as soon as Archie and I got back to my house. Lenny had really gotten himself into a fucked-up situation. This time, he really might go to jail forever. And who the hell was I to think I could do much about it—a semi-alcoholic ex-geologist with a bad attitude and freak of a dog? Yeah, that was a winning combination of attributes.

I was too restless to stay home, so I put on my vintage black leather motorcycle jacket and headed out. It was nearly 6 p.m. and I was starving. All I'd eaten since morning was coffee and beer. I needed to get something in my stomach or I'd never be able to think straight.

The Hub Cap was a short walk away. It was the only blue-collar bar in Mt. Jefferson and I was a regular there. That meant the first drink was on the house. As I opened the darkened door, the intense hit of cigarette smoke, Natty Boh and cheeseburgers were like a bump of heroin to my jangled nerves. Instinctively, my shoulders dropped an inch and my jaw unclenched. If anything could be considered my home away from home, the Hub Cap was it.

I looked down the grimy bar at the motley crew of barflies and nodded at the semi-regulars. At the near end of the bar sat Rudy, a grizzled ex-Hell's Angel turned BMW master mechanic. Rudy's days as a hard-living biker were practically gospel to Hub Cap regulars. He had done time in California for armed robbery. He'd pulled a guy's eye out with his bare hand after the guy touched his Harley, or so he claimed.

These days, Rudy lived in a mini-mansion in Carroll County with a young blonde wife and a couple of kids. He drove an SUV and went to church on Sundays. But he still had plenty of street cred and I was sure he could still beat the crap out of anyone who looked at him the wrong way. He met my eye and raised his mug in salute to another Monday night at the Hub Cap.

Next to Rudy sat Charlie O. Nobody knew who he really was. He kept showing up everyday at 5 o'clock, talking nonsense about serving in Afghanistan and smoking hashish with the Taliban. I was pretty sure he'd never set foot out of Baltimore but, if you tried to nail down details, he'd say he couldn't remember everything because he'd been gassed with Agent Orange.

A few months back, some smart-ass 25-year-old slumming it from Federal Hill started in on Charlie O. The kid kept arguing with Charlie, telling him that

Agent Orange was used in Vietnam, not Afghanistan. Charlie O. just kept listening as the guy went on, pulling out his iPhone to show Charlie O. some website about Agent Orange. When the kid looked up from his iPhone, Charlie O.—with the precision and swiftness of a pickpocket—plucked the device out of his hand, dropped it in the kid's beer and cold-cocked him. God, I loved the Hub Cap.

"Long day, Jane?" said Tom, the regular bartender. Tom was as cool as they came. He was a lean, 6' 2" rocker with a shaved head and trio of piercings in his left ear. Tonight Tom was in his usual uniform, a Bob Seger T-shirt and tight Levis. A trellis of multicolored tattoos snaked up his ropey arms.

Tom knew he was hot, but he didn't make a big deal about it. When women came on to him—which usually happened after the Ravens won or if they were fighting with their husbands—he flirted back just enough so no one's feelings got hurt. I respected that.

Tom slid a can of cold Bud into my cupped hand. "You cannot believe the kind of day I've had," I said. Tom smiled sympathetically. I gulped the beer and stifled a burp. "Monday, bloody Monday."

I slumped onto the barstool, shrugged the heavy leather jacket off my shoulders and laid it on the bar. I took another drink and sighed. Just then, the door opened.

"All hail Officer Krupke," Tom shouted. "Got a cold one coming your way, buddy."

I turned around to see who Tom was going on about. A tall Baltimore City cop walked in. I could always spot a cop a mile away. It was something about the way they walked, like they always had their uniforms on, even when they were off duty. I wasn't keen on cops, particularly when they were on my turf.

The cop sat down next to me and pulled a Camel out of his shirt pocket. Something about him was familiar, but I couldn't put my finger on it.

"Sucks to be me today," he said to Tom, taking a long drag on his cigarette and exhaling a perfect smoke ring. Then he turned toward me.

"Hi," he said, flashing me a crooked smile and pushing my jacket to the side so he could get closer to me. "I'm Don. We met this morning." Oh, shit—I knew this guy—the cop from the field. I tensed my shoulders and looked him squarely in his green eyes.

"Yeah, so what if we did?" I said flatly. Was he was going lay into me about the murder?

"Hey, relax, Miss Ronson. I'm off duty. Can I buy you a drink?"

Miss Ronson? Nobody had called me that since fourth grade.

"I'm starving; you can get me a basket of fries," I said. I didn't quite trust his motives, but I wasn't one to turn down free food and drinks. "And I'll have a rum and coke, since you're buying."

"Alcohol and greasy food. A woman after my own heart." He stamped out his cigarette and faced me full-on.

I examined his face. He wasn't cop ugly—the hardness that cops get after years of bullshit from dealing with both sides of the law. He had a buzz cut and a big dimple on his chin. He looked to be in his mid-thirties. There was a small red scar under his left eye. I could live with that.

"Sorry if I came off a little rough this morning. It's not every day that I get called to a murder in Mt. Jefferson. You never get used to seeing a body, especially if it's a kid. Seems like no one really gives a crap anymore."

So this guy wasn't a total meathead. This cop had feelings. Well, I wasn't in the mood to talk about the murder. I'd seen and heard enough for one day. I was here to drown my sorrows in cheap beer and to forget about Lenny and his problems.

"Call me Jane," I said, offering my hand. "Thanks for the food. Want some fries to go with that big police pension of yours?"

"You're a cynical one," Don said, inching even closer. I spied his police-issue Glock 22 in his waistband. "You're like that girl with the dragon tattoo—a real tough cookie. I like that."

His knees were touching mine. I started to get nervous. This guy was coming on to me, right here in the Hub Cap, my own little heart of darkness. The last time this happened, Rudy threw the guy through a plate glass window. I shot a worried glance at Rudy. He gave me a wink and shot me a double thumbs-up. "Go for it," Charlie O. mouthed and made loud kissing sounds. Jerks.

"Bring the lady an order of wings," Don said magnanimously to Tom. Jeez, this guy was pulling out all the stops. Tom plopped a plate of greasy wings in front of me. "Eat, Jane. You're too thin," he said. "Compliments of the house."

"Thanks for being the Jewish mother I never had," I laughed.

Don picked up a fry and slid it around in the gloppy pool of ketchup. "Open up, darling," he said, popping the saggy fry into my mouth. The grease and ketchup dripped down the side of my mouth as I chewed. I wiped it off with a wad of paper napkins and finished the last of my rum-and-coke.

I cracked the ice loudly between my teeth. The room began to spin. I put my hand on the bar to steady myself.

"Whoa there, hon," said Don, taking my arm. "Want to dance?"

I stumbled off the bar stool and leaned into him. He was all muscle and brawn. As we walked past

Rudy and Charlie O., I felt their eyes trained on my ass. I'd deal with those perverts later.

I staggered past the cheap pool table and onto the small dance floor. The linoleum was filthy and littered with old gum. I tried to get my bearings as another wave of dizziness hit me. Don took me in his arms, lifting me up to my full height. Cigarettes and wings scented his clothes. He was a good foot and change taller than me. My head barely reached his breastbone.

"Hit it, Tom," Don called out over his shoulder as "The Tennessee Waltz" began to play on the Hub Cap's ancient sound system. I knew this was a cheesy way to get in my pants, but after the day I'd had, I really didn't care. Don squeezed me closer. The Glock was hard against my belly. He put his hand on my butt and leaned over to kiss me. I felt an electric buzz go through my body.

"Dammit to hell," Don growled as he straightened up and pulled his buzzing cellphone out of his front pants pocket.

"Williams," he said with authority. "Yes, sergeant. OK. I'll be there."

"I've gotta run, sweetheart," he said to me in his non-cop voice, while putting his hand back on my butt. With his free hand, he slipped his business card into my jeans pocket. "There's an accident on the Beltway and it's all hands on deck. I've got to roll."

"Then you'd better get your hand off my deck," I said.

Don laughed and planted a greasy wet kiss on my lips. "I owe you some more wings," he said with a wink. He walked out of the bar to the last notes of "The Tennessee Waltz." I shot Rudy and Charlie O. the finger as I stumbled back to my bar stool, my legs rubbery from too much alcohol. Tom smiled and placed another beer in front of me. I reached into my pocket and fished out Don's card.

It read: Don Williams, Police Officer, Northwest District. I shoved the card back in my pocket. As much of a pain in the ass as cops were, you never know when a good-looking one is going to come in handy. Maybe I'd better not lose the card.

6 The Trouble with Men

Yeah, Officer Don seemed like a nice enough guy. He was pretty ripped and bought me drinks. I had no problem with that. It was the other part, the slow-dancing, almost-kissing and general good manners that upset my dysfunctional emotional cosmos.

The trouble with men was simple: they were trouble. And, since my life followed the path of least resistance when it came to men who wanted to hurt and humiliate me, I needed to keep far away from guys like Officer Don—no matter how much they said they liked me and wouldn't do me wrong.

I had a bad history with guys going 'way back.

I met Derrick in geology class my sophomore year in college. He was my lab partner, but, after the first week of class, he had other things on his mind than quartz crystals. Derrick was cute in a wanna-be tough guy way. He had a lanky frame and baby-blue eyes. He wore aviator glasses, scuffed Doc Martens and a tattered Ramones T-shirt. He fancied himself some kind of rebel, but I knew his parents—psychiatrists from Boca Raton—were sending him fat checks every month.

Derrick had a crush on me. He flirted with me before class and kept asking me out. He even left little gifts for me on our lab bench. I'd never had a guy like me before, so I was in uncharted territory when it came to behaving like a girl with a potential suitor.

I was having a rough year and Derrick distracted me from the bullshit at a large state university. The beat-down campus was located in a dried-up rust-belt city set along a polluted river. All the buildings looked the same: tired red-brick hulls that housed endless rows of dusty classrooms illuminated with hospital-strength florescent lights. The johns were filthy and smelled of cockroach spray. Sitting through lectures was like having class in a morgue with blackboards.

Attending an enormous state school had some advantages, though. I could be totally anonymous among the thousands of other students chasing business degrees. I studied geology and didn't give a rat's ass about my financial future beyond paying for pizza.

By the first week of my freshman year, I'd implemented a plan to keep myself away from as many people as possible, starting with any potential roommates. I lied on my housing application to get a coveted single room—I wrote to the dean of students explaining that I needed to get off every night to fall asleep. I said I was fine with having a roommate as long as they understood my needs. Within 24 hours, I was unpacking my duffle bag in my single room. A week later, I received a note from the university's psychological services, asking me to come in as soon as possible to discuss my "issue with manual stimulation." I wrote back saying I'd switched from masturbation to sleeping pills. That seemed to shut them up.

Derrick knew I was struggling. I told him about my shitty part-time job shelving books at the library. I napped in the air-conditioned rare book room or drank coffee in the stacks near the yards of unread doctoral dissertations. Derrick seemed sympathetic to my plight.

Because Derrick wasn't that bright, he was always asking me for help with his homework and probably wanted to cheat off my tests. He wasn't even remotely interested in vulcanism, differential sedimentation rates, hydrology or depositional analysis—all of the things that made geology fascinating for me. If you said Derrick was a dumb as a rock, you'd be insulting the rock.

Aside from looking hot, though, Derrick had another thing going for him—he had a kick-ass collection of rare punk rock CDs and albums worth thousands. I'd been addicted to punk rock from the second I first heard Johnny Rotten belt out "God save the Queen/She ain't no human being" on my ancient stereo. Punk rock suited me well; it was loud, angry and anti-social. The Sex Pistols, the Clash and the New York Dolls were my holy trinity.

One day, after he'd tanked his hydrology midterm, Derrick sidled up to me as I was shoving papers into my backpack.

"Hey, Jane, I've got some bootlegs of Cheetah Chrome and the Dead Boys live at CBGBs. You wanna hear them?"

"Sure. Just not with you," I said, slinging my backpack over my shoulder and heading out the door.

He was persistent: "I'll take you out for pizza and then we can go back to my room and check out some music. Whaddya say?"

I said yes, in part because I hadn't eaten in days, and in part because, after six weeks of turning Derrick down, I had begun to wonder if maybe I needed to give him a chance.

I met Derrick outside the library. We walked down College Road past the fraternity houses, their front lawns littered with beer bottles and broken lawn furniture. I stepped over a pile of crusted-over vomit and kicked a beer can into the gutter. I could hear the dull hum of heavy metal music coming from all sides as the frat boys geared up for another night of alcohol poisoning and looting.

At the end of the street stood Amy's, a broken-down bar that served rubbery pizza and five-dollar pitchers of watered-down beer. We sat across from each other at a wobbly table. I ordered a large pie with extra anchovies, onions and garlic—just to make sure Derrick didn't get any ideas. Derrick ordered a pitcher of beer and some hot wings. A disinterested waitress plopped the steaming pie in front of me and I scooped up a slice and shoved it in my mouth.

"Wow, you sure eat a lot for a girl," Derrick said, picking at his plate of slimy wings.

"What's that supposed to mean?" I said, taking a swig of beer from the stained plastic mug.

"Most girls just eat one slice, except for the ones who are bulimic."

"Why waste good food by throwing it up?" I said, reaching for my fourth slice. Derrick watched me chew, then screwed up his face. "You're not like any other girl I've ever met," he said.

"What kind of girl are you trying to say I am?" I challenged him.

"Just that you're super-smart, especially in chemistry, which is wicked hard. You like punk rock, you don't hang out with anyone and I know zero about your personal life."

"Nuff said, Derrick," I glowered.

"Do you have parents? Were you hatched? Alien abduction? Where did you come from? Come on, Jane, toss me some crumbs."

"All of this is on a strictly need-to-know basis and right now you do not need to know any of it," I said, polishing off the last of the pitcher. "Are you going to eat the rest of those wings?"

"Jane, I'm just trying to get to know you a little," Derrick pleaded. "You're rail-thin, but you eat like a horse. I know you can drink me and probably half of the geology department under the table. You say you hate everything, but I know you're fascinated with pyroclastic sediments; I see how your eyes light up during lectures. All I'm asking for is a chance to get to know you better."

What's the harm in opening up to someone, I thought. Isn't this what people on dates do? Maybe I should try a little bit harder to talk to people beyond monosyllabic answers. I was 19 years old and had the social skills of a turtle. It was probably time for me to act like a girl.

I wiped my hands on my jeans, folded my arms on the table, took a deep breath and began telling Derek the story of my life.

"I was born in Baltimore. My parents emigrated from Poland after World War II. My father was a chemical engineer and my mother was a bookkeeper. They were incredibly normal people who never wanted children. My birth was a complete shock.

After I was born, we moved to Mt. Jefferson. We never fit in. Too much old money there and never enough money on our end. My mother worked hard, but money was always a problem. We lived in a small apartment and I was embarrassed to bring my classmates over. They made fun of my mother's accent, her clothing and our food.

"When I was 12, my father died of cancer. My mother had to take a second job as a cleaning woman for our neighbors. She resented her second-class status every day.

"The one thing I had over the rich Mt. Jefferson girls was my brain—my grades in math and science. Those subjects come easy to me. I didn't even have to try. I'm sorry if that makes you feel bad, but it's the truth. And I've always been skinny; that's not going to change either. As for my drinking, that's not your concern.

"Why do l love rocks? I'm intrigued by igneous processes. Rocks, unlike most things in this world, are about the only substances you can count on to be silent. Rocks and minerals have stories to tell. but you have to work hard to figure out what they're saying. You solve their mysteries with your mind and a strong pickax.

"Now I'm done telling you my story. Don't bother asking any more questions."

We sat in silence. Derrick looked me like he was trying to fit all of the pieces together but couldn't. Eventually he signaled for the waitress. He tossed her a $50 bill to cover the tab. We didn't talk on the short walk back to his dorm room. I was getting nervous about going to Derrick's room. I hadn't planned on things going this far.

Derrick unlocked the heavy door to Demarest Hall and we walked up the gum-stained stairs to his third floor room. "My roommate's at his girlfriend's house tonight," he said with a wink.

With the radiator on full blast, the tiny room was suffocatingly hot. The ancient carpet reeked of sneakers and body odor. "I've got some cold beer," Derrick said, reaching into a dented refrigerator and extracting two Budweisers. I held the can against my head. I'd never told someone so much about me in so short a time. The sudden self-disclosure nauseated me. My temples throbbed and I was sweating like a racehorse.

Derrick put on a Talking Heads CD and started pogo-ing around the room as the heavy bass chords to "Psycho Killer" boomed in my ears.

"Turn that fucking music down!" I shouted. My head felt like it was going to explode. Derrick fiddled with something at his desk.

"I've got some great blow if you want. It's from my source in Miami," he said as he hopped from foot to foot.

Before I could respond, Derrick had already laid down three lines of cocaine on his Introduction to

Physical Geology textbook and was busily snorting them.

"I'm leaving," I said, hoping he wouldn't notice the panic in my voice.

"Psycho Killer, que'est-ce que c'est ... fa fa fa fa fa fa fa fa fa ..." Derrick screamed from across the room.

I got off the saggy dorm bed and slammed the CD player's off button. Derrick was still jerking his body around as if he was having a grand mal seizure.

"Don't go, you just got here. I want you to stay."

"Some other time," I said. My T-shirt was soaked with sweat and my heart fluttered like the wings of a butterfly trapped in a jar.

Derrick moved toward me with alarming speed. He grabbed my wrists and pulled me against him, smashing his slobbery lips against my clenched mouth.

"Jane, you're a hard nut, but I'm going to crack you." He twisted my arms behind his back. I brought my knee up to his groin. He dropped my arms and exhaled in pain. I feinted right and moved left. The door was just a yard away. But I hadn't accounted for the double locks. How could I have been so stupid? This was like every bad movie on cable TV, where the girl is locked up with a psycho and can't escape. Why did I let myself fall into this moron's trap?

I was fumbling with the top lock when Derrick came at me from behind. The coke made him more powerful than I expected. He seemed like a super-villain from a comic book. He hooked his arm around my skinny waist and flung me across the room. I landed hard against the wall and fell onto his bed. I started to pass out. My ears rang and my vision telescoped. Derrick moved toward me like a wolf closing in on his prey. I tried to stand up but fell back against the wall.

Derrick flung himself on me. He pressed his belly against mine and pushed his hands under my shirt. I wriggled my legs and tossed my head from side to side to try to avoid his drooling lips. He slapped my face and hissed: "Hold the fuck still before I kill you."

My cheek burned as if lava had been poured on it. In an instant, my sympathetic nervous system jumped to attention and my whole body became alert. Out of the corner of my eye, I saw the glint of something metal on Derrick's desk. It was his rock hammer. If only I could reach it, I could do some serious damage.

"Oh, Derrick, I have been waiting for this moment," I said sarcastically, twisting my body toward the desk.

"I'll bet you're some kind of freaky virgin," Derrick slurred, his breath thick with anger and lust.

I stretched my arm out just far enough to grab the end of the hammer. Just as I was about to grasp it, Derrick pushed me to the left. The maniac was trying to flip me over! I momentarily lost my grip on the hammer as I fought to stay on my back. "We're going back door now," said Derrick, unzipping his fly with one hand and holding me down with the other.

Derrick was on top of me with his face pressed against mine. I knew I had only one chance to get this right. I sucked in my breath and screamed as loud as I could in his ear. The sound shocked him and he momentarily loosened his grip on my hip. That was all the opening I needed. I rocketed myself into a sitting position and punched him squarely in the eye. "Shit!" Derrick screamed, covering his eye with both hands.

I reached for the hammer. This time, I was able to grasp it. I shoved Derrick off me and wobbled to my feet. He stood up, his eye now swollen and runny. "Little Jane's got herself a hammer," he said mockingly.

"Don't fuck with me, Derrick. Don't move a muscle or I'll smash your head open."

"Whoa there," Derrick said pulling his pants up. "Take it easy, Jane. I was only trying to have some fun with you."

"Yeah, this was big fun ... if you're a rapist," I said, keeping my eyes on him. "Now stand in the corner with your face to the wall. No fast moves."

Derrick backed away. "Easy," I cooed, gripping the hammer even tighter. I was afraid to turn my back so I side-stepped toward the door. When I was halfway to the door, Derrick stopped backing away and began moving toward me. I felt him shadowing me muscle by muscle. There was no way I was going to get out the door without someone getting hurt.

"This is a hammer. I think you know what it's used for," I said in a steely tone.

I lifted the hammer to shoulder height so I could strike quickly. "Sit and stay, Derrick. I'm going to leave now and this will be forgotten."

I inched closer toward the door and put my hand on the knob. How was I going to manage both the handle and the locks with just one hand? Derrick must have read my mind. I sensed him move even before I felt him lunge toward me. I lifted the hammer higher and brought it down on his right shoulder. I heard a crack and a scream.

"You bitch," he yelped.

Derrick grabbed me as I tried to open the door. This time, his grip wasn't as strong. I was still fumbling with the locks when he body-slammed me into the door. I lifted the hammer and drove the pickax end into the side of Derrick's neck. He dropped to his knees. I brought the hammer down for the last time—a direct blow to his other shoulder. Now he had matching wounds–I always did like symmetry.

Derrick was quiet. He looked up at me with pleading eyes.

"Why, Jane, why? I just wanted to be your friend."

"With friends like you, let's hope I never have any enemies."

I dropped the hammer, unlocked the door and ran like hell.

7
I ♥ New York

Derrick was in the hospital with two broken collarbones. He said he got hurt falling out of a tree; I guess he didn't want to face up to being a sexual predator. I couldn't risk seeing him again, even though he sent me a note saying he wouldn't press charges if I agreed to be his girlfriend. The idea of getting locked up for defending myself against a rapist didn't sit well with me. And I didn't have any money, so hiring a lawyer to file charges against Derrick wasn't on the table, either. I thought about trying to shake down Derrick's rich parents, but they'd probably sue me.

Under the circumstances, continuing with school wasn't an option. So I chose the path of least resistance. I dropped out of school and bought a one-way bus ticket to New York City. Lenny was studying photography at NYU. He was the only person I trusted enough to tell about the Derrick fiasco and who wouldn't care if I crashed on his floor until I figured out my next move.

The night before I left, I slept on a bench in the freezing Greyhound bus terminal. I hadn't eaten in two days and my whole body shook with fear and hunger. All my worldly possessions were stuffed in an army duffle bag as I boarded the bus and sat in the back, with my face leaning against the dirty window.

The bus hummed along the New Jersey Turnpike. I tried to think about Bruce Springsteen songs, but instead of romantic Jersey boys on motorcycles who would sweep me off my feet and take me to Mexico, all I saw in the darkness were oil refineries and semis.

I fell asleep somewhere between Elizabeth and Jersey City. The air stank of chemicals and fetid swamps.

My bus arrived in New York at 5 a.m. and disgorged its half-asleep passengers into the upper reaches of the Port Authority bus station. The enormous station looked like the set of a Fellini movie, with a cast of characters speaking in Brooklyn accents and overflowing with New York fuck-you attitudes. The station was coated with a thick layer of grime on top of filth.

I stepped in a pile of fresh vomit spewed by a drunk sprawled on the stairwell. "Ya got something for me, girlie?" he muttered as I hurried by. I felt like I'd walked into a living, breathing Hieronymus Bosch painting—all the crazy people in the world had been shaken, stirred and dropped into one roiling cesspool of humanity.

I descended the rickety escalator to the main floor and threaded my way past the zombie army of drunks and homeless people. My bladder was bursting, but one look at the junkies nodding off in the restrooms and the trannies putting on their make-up in the cracked mirrors convinced me that I'd be better off keeping my legs crossed.

I pushed the smeared revolving glass door and exited with a whoosh of air onto Eighth Avenue. The city was just coming to life. I inhaled the heady scent of exhaust and the nervous energy of early morning in midtown Manhattan. Cabs flew by like swarms of pissed-off wasps. In the cold pre-dawn, the lights on the skyscrapers twinkled like sooty stars.

With my last dollar, I bought a cup of black coffee from a 24-hour diner, then slung my duffle bag over my shoulder and hiked downtown to find Lenny. It promised to be a long walk.

Along Eighth Avenue, I passed tiny newsstands with the *New York Times* stacked next to girlie magazines and cheap gee-gaws. Vendors hawking enormous pretzels stood on every other corner. I walked past cheap souvenir stands and XXX theaters with broken-down marquees.

I couldn't take my eyes off the people who jostled past me. A mix of hostile co-existence floated in the air, the look of people's faces read: "Don't screw me and I won't screw you." I passed a guy in an "I ♥ New

York" sweatshirt walking a pit bull with a spiked collar.

A turbaned taxi driver pulled up next to me and a woman in a head-to-toe fur coat stepped out of the cab. She glided by me like some exotic creature passing an alley cat.

I'd never seen so many new things in so little time. New York City felt as foreign as Bombay and as accessible as Mars. I felt like my provincial life in Baltimore was light years behind me.

I wasn't sure where NYU was, but I wasn't going to risk asking anyone and looking as if I just fell off the turnip truck. After wandering around Greenwich Village for an hour, I finally located Lenny's building. John V. Lindsey Hall was one of NYU's new dormitories, all of 25 stories, with three elevators and a well-appointed lobby.

I'd never seen a doorman before and wasn't sure if I needed to tip him. The guy looked at me and shook his head dismissively as I handed him a quarter.

I took the elevator to the fifth floor and located Lenny's room. He finally opened the door after I'd been pounding on it for about three minutes. He didn't seem surprised to see me. "Hey, Jane," he said, trying to hug me. I pushed past him. Why did Lenny always want to touch me? What was he going to do next, try to kiss me?

"What happened to you?" he asked with un-abashed concern. "You look like you haven't slept in a bed in years. Are you staying for a while? I can run a bath for you."

I dropped my bag on the unswept floor and collapsed onto Lenny's stinky futon. I was exhausted from my all-night bus ride and smelled like a pile of dog shit wrapped in a pissed-on sweater.

"I don't want a bath," I snorted. "I need a cigarette and a place to lie low for a few days. Are you cool with that?"

"Sure. You know I always have room for you. I love you, Jane. You're my only cousin and family's got to stick together."

There it was again, that feeling that I'd been trying to get rid of since I was little, the feeling that I was connected to someone—that I was responsible for someone's emotional baggage. Ever since the debacle at the camera store, Lenny and I had had an unspoken understanding that we would be there for each other—anytime, anyplace.

I still felt uneasy about it. I wished I could just exist in a world without any complications. My life was already enough of a mess. But I was all out of options. I hated to admit it, but I needed Lenny now more than I ever did. He was my only lifeline to keeping my sanity and staying one step away from sleeping in the street.

I pulled a half-smoked cigarette out of my pocket and put it to my lips. I let the fatigue of the last 24 hours fully seep into my bones. I was only 19 years old and my life was in the toilet. I was broke, homeless and battered. I owned one pair of underwear and had zero prospects for my future. Things were looking pretty vacant, to quote the lyrics of the Sex Pistols.

I found a pack of matches and lit the cigarette. I started pacing past Lenny, who sat on the floor surrounded by his cameras. "I don't really like people smoking here. It discolors my prints," Lenny said. "But I know you really need to do it. Just please don't smoke close to my pictures."

Lenny's walls were plastered with black-and-white contact sheets and 8 x 12 glossy prints. I took a long drag and exhaled a chain of smoke rings toward the ceiling in a gesture of respect for Lenny's work.

I held the cigarette behind me and moved closer to the pictures. He'd captured couples kissing in Washington Square Park—probably the closest Lenny had gotten to sex in his life. There must have been 40 shots of the same couple making out under the massive arch along the park's northern entrance.

I scanned the pictures taped to the other white walls: shots of wizened old black men engrossed in chess games, half-naked kids joyfully splashing in a fountain and acid-tripping hippies sitting cross-legged in the grass strumming acoustic guitars.

Lenny had captured the zeitgeist of the park, a juxtaposition of the crazy and the sublime. Nobody played it safe in New York; you could have a junkie sitting next to a yuppie and, within five minutes, they'd be fast friends.

"You ever think of earning some money from your pictures?"

Lenny looked up at me with the same goofy smile I remembered from our childhood.

"Nah. I love just walking around taking pictures of people. Want to go to Washington Square Park and do some people-watching?"

It's not like I had anything else to do. Lenny slung two cameras around his neck and stuffed a candy bar into his pocket. I followed him the three short blocks to the park. Just like the old days, I thought; me and Lenny and those damn cameras.

It was November, and patches of ice and dirty snow lingered at the park's edges. I stamped my feet and rubbed my hands together. I wished I had something warmer than my denim jacket. Lenny patrolled the perimeter of the park, snapping pictures of pigeons pecking at trash that people had thrown into the empty fountains. A few junkies shivered on the broken benches, waiting for NYU students to buy nickel bags.

I felt something sharp dig into the back of my knee. I looked down: a black-and-white puppy was sinking its teeth into my pant leg and tugging against my jeans with all of its might. The puppy was as skinny as an anorexic rat. My first thought was to kick it away. I only had one pair of jeans and didn't have the money to buy even a pair of socks, much less a new pair of pants.

I counted to 10 to calm myself down, then detached the growling puppy. The beast had torn an apple-sized hole and was looking to do more damage. It licked my face and wagged its tail as I bent down to pull its razor teeth away from the fabric. There was no owner in sight.

"Go home, you little brat," I warned the puppy. "I don't need any of your bullshit."

The puppy sat at my feet and shivered. Crap.

I searched my pocket for a scrap of food. All I found was some stale gum and a broken cigarette.

"I've got nothing for you, varmint. Go find another sucker."

I walked toward Lenny with the puppy trotting behind me.

"You got a puppy," Lenny beamed. "What are you going to call it?" he said as he snapped frame and after frame of the puppy.

"I hate animals," I said, trying not to look at the puppy, who was now whimpering.

"Let's take him back to my apartment and get some food into him," Lenny chirped. "He can't weigh more than 10 pounds. Pick him up and let's all get out of the cold."

I looked at Lenny, then at the puppy. They both stared at me with the same pleading expression.

"OK, OK," I said, knowing that I was outnumbered. I scooped up the puppy. It immediately fell asleep in my arms.

"Stop taking my picture!" I huffed as the puppy gently snored. I felt its little heart beating against my chest; its pink nose twitched.

"Just a few more shots, Jane. Hold the puppy closer to your chest like a baby."

"Like I know anything about babies, you moron."

Lenny put down his camera and smiled. "I think you just may have to keep him. I can't be the only thing in your life you need to take care of."

I couldn't tell Lenny that holding the puppy in my arms felt good. That it made me feel powerful in a way that slinging a hammer didn't. I could protect this little creature, and, in return, he would look out for me.

"I'm calling him Archie," I declared. "And he's all mine."

Murder in the Dog Park

8 Time to Bail

I was sound asleep and really didn't want to wake up enough to take a phone call, but sometimes that's just life. I growled something that must have sounded almost like "Hello."

"Is this Miss Jane Ronson?"

"Yeah, speaking. Who the hell is this? I'm in bed and it's fucking 3 o'clock in the morning."

"This is Jerome from Bad Boyz Bail Bonds. Your cousin Lenny Pryzgocki is in custody. He's been charged with manslaughter. The judge just posted bail. You're looking at a $10,000 surety bond to get him out of Central. I prefer cash."

I was wide awake, but I couldn't talk.

"You still there?"

I flung my cellphone across the room. I didn't know which was pissing me off more, that Lenny was arrested for manslaughter or that I was on the hook for $10,000 to spring him.

I'd quit smoking after I started kickboxing a few years back. But calls from bail bondsmen at 3 a.m. call for exceptions. I got out of bed and rummaged through my room until I found a stale pack of Winstons in my night table. I lit up and called Bad Boyz.

"Jerome speaking."

"It's Jane Ronson. Sorry I had to hang up so fast, I needed a moment."

"Happens all the time, lady. So, are you gonna post?"

"Yeah, I'm good for it."

"We're right next to the Supermax prison. You can't miss our sign, it's pink and yellow and reads 'Get Outta Jail for Free—Almost.' We're here 24 hours."

Archie nuzzled my leg. I sat down on the hard wooden floor and scratched his wedge-shaped head. I imagined a few bad guys from North Avenue had already taken a few swings at Lenny, or worse. I had to get that money—and soon. Lenny wasn't the kind of guy who could last more than a few hours in jail. He was probably sitting in a corner bawling already.

I had $3,000 in cash stashed away for emergencies. I made most of it last summer when I found a Baltimore City Council member's wife advertising her sexual services on Craigslist. I called up just to make sure that "happy ending" didn't mean a smile and a Tootsie Roll. Let's just say that Council member Hardy made me very happy with a $3,000 cash payment to keep my mouth shut. I took the $3,000 and jammed it into my underwear.

I still needed to round up $7,000 within the next few hours to make Lenny's bail. I sat down on the couch and blew some smoke rings. Nicotine always helped me think straight. I took inventory of all my worldly possessions. My crappy Toyota wasn't worth more than a grand at most. I didn't own a house and I didn't have jewelry. I considered breaking into the manor house and making off with some of rare coins I had found in the false bottom of a desk. But thievery wasn't my thing.

If I could just get Lenny out of jail, maybe I could figure a way to make these charges disappear. Lenny had definitely been set up by the Legg-Alexanders. Money and class always won in the end. If I could get Lenny free, I'd nail those parasites once and for all.

I looked at the framed black-and-white photograph of Washington Square above my bed. Lenny gave me the photo a few years back, after I admired it. He told me he'd won second place in some SoHo art gallery contest for best photograph of an urban park. The next day an agent called Lenny up, all excited. The agent offered him $15,000 for the picture and a $50,000 signing bonus to exclusively represent him. He turned her down flat.

"I'm a serious photojournalist, not a trained monkey who takes pictures for people who buy pictures to match their couches," he proudly told me.

"You don't have a pot to piss in and you just turned down more than $50,000 because you've got a hang-up about couches?" I screamed. "Way to go, Rembrandt!"

I studied the photograph again. I liked the way the shadows fell like long gloves over the people walking under the arch. A gray cloud with scalloped edges hung in the otherwise bare sky.

I lifted the photograph off the wall and leaned it against the couch. Ebay was going to take it from here. I figured I could get a couple of hundred dollars for it.

"Sorry, buddy," I said to Archie. "Gonna have to say bye-bye to Lenny's masterpiece."

An idea clicked. Lenny's cameras. He must have had close to 100 vintage cameras and God know how much camera equipment in his apartment. All of that gear had to be worth something. I could pawn the cameras on Greenmount Avenue. Pawnshops were always on the prowl for stuff like that.

I grabbed the spare key to Lenny's apartment. Archie jumped up. His tail thumped against the bedpost. We drove the short distance to Lenny's lair. He lived in the basement of a run-down apartment off Park Heights Avenue. On Saturday mornings, crowds of Orthodox Jews walked to the nondescript synagogues in the neighborhood.

Lenny's place reminded me of a tenement with its smells, cacophony of squabbling neighbors and general air of despair. A large rat was perched on the edge of a hulking dumpster overflowing with trash. I couldn't blame Lenny for living in that kind of place;

it was cheap and he could come and go without too much notice. And it was practically windowless, dark even on the brightest days—the perfect hideout for a broke photographer with no friends.

I flipped on the overhead light and dropped Archie's leash. I hadn't been over in awhile. I was shocked that the apartment wasn't the pigsty I remembered from my visit at the holidays. Granted, there were the requisite towers of pizza boxes and fast-food wrappers on almost every surface, but I could still see my feet. That was hopeful.

While Archie hunted for half-eaten burgers and decomposing mice, I started loading cameras into my duffle bag. After I'd filled the sack with everything I could see in plain sight, I opened Lenny's bedroom closet. It was stuffed to the gills with crap. I'd need a backhoe to clear it out. Archie yelped as a cardboard box dropped like a stone from the top shelf and crashed onto his front paw. He limped into the tiny kitchen to lick grease off the floor. "Stick to the kitchen, Archie. It's the safest room in this construction zone," I said.

I bent down and looked at what was in the cardboard box. It was loaded with more cameras: old Minolta SRT MC-IIs, Polaroid Land 240s, a handful of tiny Kodak Instamatics and a bulky Bell & Howell reel-to-reel Super 8 projector. I dumped a load of stinky underwear out of Lenny's laundry basket and started filling it with cameras. As I reached in the cardboard box for the last of the cameras, my hand hit something hard and smooth. At first I thought it was a camera case, but it was the wrong size and shape. It was definitely a case of some kind. I picked it up and started sweating. The case was made of dense, dark wood with elaborate brass hinges. It was a gun case.

I carefully snapped open the box and held my breath: Inside was a gleaming Smith & Wesson .38 snubnose Chief's Special Airweight—the kind of heat Humphrey Bogart and Jimmy Cagney used to wave around in the old gangster movies. What the hell was Lenny doing with a piece like this?

I wiped my fingerprints off the .38 and gingerly put it back in the gun case. If the cops searched the apartment, they'd be sure to find the weapon. Like Lenny needed any more trouble. I put the gun case in the bottom of the laundry basket and covered it up with some sheets.

It was almost daylight and I needed to move fast, before anyone saw me leave. I searched Lenny's desk for any other valuables. Under a notebook in the bottom-most drawer, I found five thick wads of hundred-dollar bills held together with red rubber bands—about $2,000. I didn't have time to considered how Lenny came to be sitting on a pile of cash like that. The only thing I knew was that I'd need every penny of Lenny's rainy-day fund to give to Jerome the bail bondsman. I shoved the bills in my knapsack.

Archie yapped at the front door, warning me that it was time to go. He had the remnants of a Big Mac wrapper stuck to his muzzle. "Archie, I sure wish you were as good at finding money as you are at scrounging leftovers. Get in the car. We're headed downtown to bail Lenny's ass out of jail. I've got some business to take care of with a guy called Jerome."

The morning rush hour traffic was in full swing when I turned onto the Jones Falls Expressway. I loaded a Nine Inch Nails CD and cranked up my cheap speakers. A silver Audi zoomed up to tailgate me as I merged into the traffic. The guy turned on his brights and sat on my bumper. Archie jumped into the back seat and snarled at the driver through the rear window. I flipped the guy the bird. After a minute, the car found a sliver of space and rocketed around me. I saw a "Tompkins Lacrosse" sticker on his window. Yeah, today was just getting better and better.

I exited at Guilford Avenue and turned into a decrepit strip mall. Bad Boyz Bail Bonds sat in between a walk-in drug testing clinic and Miss Dupree's Wigs and Extension Boutique. Across the street, a trio of homeless men in ripped parkas stood ghost-like in the shadow of the Jones Falls Expressway, huddled around a barrel and warming their hands over a weak fire.

I hit the buzzer and walked inside. Archie stayed in the car to guard Lenny's gear. The place reminded me of a Jiffy Lube waiting room crossed with a minimum security prison. Security cameras were mounted on the ceiling and an autographed Dog the Bounty Hunter poster hung on the wall. A TV played the "Today" show and the coffee machine had a fresh pot brewing.

I helped myself to a mug of jet fuel and rapped on the Plexiglass separating the waiting area from the back office. A few seconds later, a very large man opened the door.

"You must be Miss Ronson," he said, offering a surprisingly delicate hand.

"And you must be Jerome," I said, squeezing my coffee mug and keeping my other hand in my jeans pocket.

Jerome and I sized each other up. He was a good foot-and-a-half taller than me, with a dyed blond pompadour, overly plucked eyebrows and pale pink lipstick. He wore '80s-style acid-washed, high-waisted jeans. He could have been the love child of Elvis and Cher.

"Miss Ronson, your cousin's in a heap of trouble," he said, after inviting me to sit on a pink leather couch.

"Tell me something I don't already know," I said, downing the last of my coffee. "I've got most of the bail money for you. Will you work with me?"

"Show me what you've got and we'll see where this goes."

I'd seen this guy before. Only he wasn't exactly looking like a guy when I'd last come across him during transvestite bingo night at the Hippo Club in Mt. Vernon.

"Jerome, are you ...?"

"Not many people catch on so fast, Miss Ronson," he smiled, batting his blue eyes at me. "Yes, I also go by Geraldine LaRue. You may have seen me on the Big Boyz float at the Gay Pride Parade. I throw pens to the audience and wear impossible heels. You have no idea how much I suffer for my art. Like Miss Dolly Parton says, it costs a fortune to look cheap. I also own the wig shop next door and design a line of ball gowns for cross-dressers. But for now, let's talk about Lenny."

I relaxed. Jerome and I could do business. We were both freaks in a world that didn't cut people like us much slack. Jerome was on my side.

I dumped all the money out my knapsack.

"Start counting," I said as I pulled bills out of my underwear and tossed them on Jerome's desk next to the framed picture of Donna Summer. "I'll be right back."

I walked to the car to fetch the laundry basket with the cameras and the .38. Archie was curled up in the back seat, snoring.

When I returned to the office, Jerome was perched on the edge of his desk, delicately filing his French-tipped manicured nails.

"You're short a few thousand, girlfriend," he said, inspecting his pinky finger. "You best put those dirty clothes elsewhere. This isn't a laundromat."

"Hang on, Jerome," I said. I pulled off the sheet to reveal the cameras. "These are vintage cameras. People will pay crazy money for them. You can get $500 each for them. Go ahead, look them up on eBay. The whole basket-full is worth at least $2,000."

Jerome picked up a 500C Hasselblad and started fiddling with it.

I pulled the gun case out of the laundry basket.

"Check this out," I said, smiling like the Cheshire Cat as I handed it to him.

Jerome ceremoniously unsnapped the hinges. The box popped open with a sound like biting into a fresh apple. "Oh, sweet Jesus," he whistled, picking up the gun and caressing its handle. "Be still, my beating heart. My first gun was a Smithie. I am such a sentimental girl when it comes to .38s."

"So, are we good?" I asked.

"Not yet, sweetheart. You know I can't take this gun. And I don't know nothing about cameras. I deal in cold, hard cash. Besides, my women's intuition is telling me that you need to hang onto the Smithie. You never know when you might need to use this baby for real."

I did some quick calculations. With the cameras and cash, I'd have about $8,000—still two grand short of Lenny's bail.

Jerome must have read my mind. "Tell you what. I don't normally do this but I'm going to extend a professional courtesy and kick in the remaining $2,000. You probably don't know this, but Lenny has been helping me with my modeling portfolio. We're almost done with the nudie shots and, let me tell you, he's one hell of a photographer. He really knows how to flatter a woman's figure, especially a pre-op tranny such as moi."

This was way too much information for 7:30 in the morning.

"I'll spring Lenny in a few hours and deliver him to your house by lunchtime," Jerome said, re-applying his lipstick. "Now get your skinny ass out of this part of town, Miss Jane."

9 Bad to be Good

Jerome was right; it was time to bail. I needed to get some rest and to plan my next move before Lenny was sprung from jail.

I lit up a cigarette, blew a stream of smoke rings and yawned before heading back to Mt. Jefferson.

By the time I reached my front door, I was so exhausted I didn't even have the energy to pee. I had just enough strength to kick off my jeans before doing a face plant into the sheets. Archie jumped on the bed, circled around three times and organized himself into a fetal dog position. He let out a low moan and fell into a snoring ball. I conked out right along with him.

I woke up at 2 p.m. feeling like my head was packed with nails and my body had been tortured by a gang of sadistic midgets. My jaws were clenched like a pit bull on steroids and my temples throbbed like a lowrider at an intersection.

I slid out of bed slowly and staggered toward the bathroom. To say I looked like hell would be a compliment. My short brown hair stuck up like a poor man's Mohawk.

I sat on the toilet to pee, trying not to think. I knew that if I didn't do something drastic *today*, there's no way to save Lenny from going to prison for the rest of his pathetic life.

At least something went right: As promised, Jerome had sprung Lenny from jail and hand-delivered him to my doorstep.

Lenny sat on my couch, inhaling a double cheese-burger like a Death Row inmate with his last supper.

"It was awful, Jane," he said in between gobbling french fries and slurping on a bucket-sized Coke. "There was only one toilet in the middle of the room and you can't use it because there's no door. Please don't let them ever put me in jail again."

Archie sat at Lenny's feet, tracking the movement of Lenny's hand from the McDonald's bag to his mouth. A thin trickle of drool hung out of the left side of his muzzle. "Give Archie a fry," I ordered. Lenny obediently offered Archie a fry, then shoved two more into his own mouth.

"Now listen up," I began, cracking my knuckles. "You are now under house arrest. That means you are going to park yourself in my house and stay out of trouble. You got that?"

"Uh, huh," Lenny nodded.

"You are not to go to your apartment. Do you understand?"

"Can I watch TV?"

I switched on Judge Judy and left Lenny sprawled on the couch with a bag of chocolate chip cookies and a quart of milk. I had some serious work to do, and I needed Lenny to be in a deep food coma and stay out of my hair.

After I was laid off from my last job as a geologist, I couldn't find work. So I bought a used laptop and decided to teach myself a new skill: computer hacking. I'd always been pretty good with technical stuff. The summer of my sophomore year in high school, I rebuilt a VW engine, to the astonishment of my boyfriend. I figured this couldn't be much harder.

Computers didn't intimidate me, and I was definitely a white-hat hacker—the kind who didn't try to take down major networks or anything malicious. I was just naturally curious and I needed money. Over the years, I found people who would pay for my services, usually semi-sleazy private detective agencies who needed the goods on cheating husbands and scofflaws who didn't pay their condominium fees.

It wasn't too hard to lasso adulterers, especially the ones who seemed to want to get caught. Once I got a case, I'd hack into the target's computer and install a program that tracked every keystroke they made and allowed me to see pictures from their computer's camera.

Almost all of these scum bags congregated in the same cyberchat cesspools and nasty websites that offered cheap sex with girls, boys and everything in between. It turned my stomach every time

I'd find one of these so-called upright family men, whose screensaver picture showed him on vacation at Bethany Beach with his arms around his wife and tanned kids playing in the sand, trolling for hookers and blow jobs on the Internet. And it didn't take a genius to hack into their cellphones and read their text messages to Crystal, Nikita or Angel asking for the price of a three-way and then trying to bargain it down.

Once I heard Lenny and Archie snoring, I flipped open my MacBook Pro and got busy. I'd recently downloaded some Linux software that promised to crack any kind of encryption in less than five seconds.

The plan was to find out everything I could about Brice Legg-Alexander, Jared's asshole lawyer father. Given that he'd spawned a sociopathic murderer of a son, I knew this guy was bad news; I just didn't know how low he'd sunk. I ran a few basic search programs to locate his cellphone and computers. I decided to start by checking for outstanding parking tickets.

Even high-priced lawyers can't get out of parking tickets. You could always track someone through the double parking fines he'd racked up.

I clipped my fingernails as my screen filled with information about Brice Legg-Alexander. First I checked the keystroke records for his home computer the past three months. Nothing too suspicious; just a few online poker sites and the occasional Google search for "tantric sex." Next I looked at his personal cellphone. There was nothing incriminating in his text messages save for some back-and-forthing about scoring tickets for Ravens games and bullshit about an upcoming trip to Paris for his anniversary.

I stayed with it. I knew this guy was dirty and I was going to keep digging until I found a way to out him.

I got up to pee. When I got back, the computer screen was blank. "Shit. This is a fucking lousy time for a crash." It was just resting for the moment, though. Suddenly, the screen came back to life. It was filled with names with dollar signs next to them, followed by an alpha-numeric code. I felt like Neo when he finally sees what's behind the Matrix. But what the hell was I looking at? I rubbed my eyes and re-focused my attention.

I was looking at a spreadsheet. It must have been from a device I couldn't locate with my initial programs. I checked the background codes. It was from an iPhone registered to "D. Howard Mellman." That must be Legg-Alexander's alias, I thought. This is where he's hiding his porn.

And there it was, in a tidy Excel spreadsheet—all the names and prices of the hookers Legg-Alexander had seen in the past three years. Dozens of women, and even some boys, all with the sex acts performed and prices for each act in left-justified columns.

The guy was an anal-retentive freak. Who tracks this stuff except someone who knows his way around prostitutes and likes to make a dollar scream?

I hit "print" and started copying the spreadsheet into a Word document. Then I cross-matched D. Howard Mellman's IP address with Legg-Alexander's. I needed to prove that they belonged to the same person if I had any chance of getting to him.

I fished the last cookie out of the bag and waited. The screen fluttered. I hit the return button and held my breath. Bingo. It matched.

I had him. Brice Legg-Alexander was toast, and soon his son was going to be, too. But my work was only just beginning.

I tiptoed into my bedroom and reached under my bed. I pulled out the wooden box with Lenny's gun and placed it on my mattress. It had been a long time since I fired a gun. After the incident with Derrick, I bought a cheap .38 special at the pawn shop and logged some time at the gun range. I was a pretty good shot, but never had enough money to buy much ammo or upgrade to a big-girl gun.

The Smith & Wesson felt good in my hand. It was hefty and cool to the touch. I put on my leather motorcycle jacket and carefully put the gun in my inner breast pocket. I didn't load it. I knew that the gun was going to be intimidating enough to Legg-Alexander without having to blow a hole in his head, or so I hoped.

I put the printout in my backpack and slipped out the door.

I knew from Legg-Alexander's last text message that he was going to the Mt. Jefferson Tavern for happy hour. I usually avoided the Tavern like the plague. It was infested with corpulent, aging frat boys who still talked about bullshit like beer pong and trips to Daytona for spring break. They liquored up at the Tavern and ogled the leggy blonde drug reps.

I took my time walking down the hill to the Tavern. Once I got there, I cracked my knuckles as I stood outside for a minute to get my bearings. The Tavern was packed.

I peered through the big picture window to see if I could spot Legg-Alexander and saw him sitting at the end of the bar, talking to a woman and nursing a beer.

I entered the Tavern and pushed my way past the knots of sloshed couples at the two-tops and headed straight for the bar. I stood just behind Legg-Alexander. He didn't notice me. He seemed entranced by the woman, a busty redhead drinking a martini.

"Brice Legg-Alexander," I said, gripping his right shoulder.

He turned his heavy frame around. His eyes were bloodshot. He was half-drunk and looked like he was well on the way to passing out or puking.

"Who are you?" he slurred. "How do you know me?"

"I know more about you than you can possibly imagine. We are going outside for a private talk," I said, pushing his beer aside. "Beat it, sister."

The redhead shot me a dirty look and backed away.

"What the hell is this?" said Legg-Alexander. "What do you want?"

"Outside now, or else the whole Tavern is going to know about your appetite for prostitutes and your murderer of a son."

That got his attention. Without a fuss, he got up and we walked outside.

"Where are we going?" he asked. I sensed the fear building in him. Power freaks like this never liked it when the tables were turned. I had to stay in control or I would lose any advantage I'd gained.

"Just keep walking," I said with authority as I steered him toward the woods on the far side of the light-rail station. "Now you can stop."

The station was nearly deserted. I waited until the last commuters got into their cars and pulled away. Then I took the gun out of my jacket and pointed it at him. He didn't flinch.

"If you want money, take my wallet. There's $300 in cash. I can get more," he pleaded.

"I don't want your damn money, Brice."

I kept the gun pointed at him as I slid my backpack off, unzipped it and took out the printout of Legg-Alexander's close encounters of the sleazy kind.

"I'm going to spare you the effort of reading this," I said, holding the printout in front of me. It's a record of all the prostitutes and lewd acts you've paid for over the last year. Don't even begin to ask if it's real or not."

I paused. Legg-Alexander looked like a dog that's been scolded for peeing on the rug.

"Does the name D. Howard Mellman ring a bell?" I continued. "You know what you've done. If you deny any of it, I will start by shooting you in the knee."

"You know you could ruin me," he finally said.

"That's the idea, Brice. The same way your family is ruining mine."

"What do you mean?"

"I think you know my cousin Lenny Ronson, the guy you and your wife are framing for the murder in the dog park. I know your psycho son is the real killer."

I gave him a second to process that information.

"You can't prove anything," he said in a lawyerly voice.

"Don't get smart with me, Brice," I said, cocking the gun. "I have no problem hand-delivering this printout to every journalist, blogger, TV station and cop in Baltimore. And your wife will get a copy, too, along with your law partners."

He slumped. I knew I had him.

"OK, let's make a deal," he said.

"No deal, Brice. I call the shots and here's what you're going to do. You will talk to whoever it was you conspired with to frame Lenny for the murder. Call in your dirty favors with judges, cops—whoever is in your pocket. You will get them to drop all the charges against Lenny. I want my cousin's record wiped clean as a whistle. You have 24 hours to get it done. Are we clear?"

I could see Legg-Alexander scheming. He wasn't taking me seriously. It was time to implement plan B.

I stepped closer to him. As he started to back up, I unleashed a roundhouse kick to his solar plexus that dropped him like a stone. He never saw it coming.

I stood over him as he peered up at me. Then I put my foot on his groin and stomped hard. He howled like a baby cougar.

"Did you think I was kidding?" I said, giving him an extra punch in the ribcage. I knelt down beside him and shoved the gun against his jugular vein. His eyes bugged out of his head and he was sweating.

"I am 100-percent serious about exposing you as a freak. And I expect you will be equally as serious about clearing Lenny's record. Now I will ask you for a final time: Are we clear?"

Legg-Alexander nodded shakily. "I'll do whatever you ask."

"Stay put, Brice," I said as I put the gun back in my jacket and picked up my backpack. "Wait 10 minutes. Then you can go back to the Tavern," I said, tossing a $5 bill at him. "Here, have a beer on me."

I walked away smiling to myself. Yeah, sometimes a girl's just gotta be bad to be good.

10 Light and Sweet

It looked like I had most of my bases covered, but you never know. I figured Legg-Alexander's father would weasel out of his promise to help get Lenny off the hook if he had half a chance. You could never count on a lawyer to be anything but crooked and self-serving.

Yeah, I had special plans for him that involved humiliation and physical pain way beyond the ass-kicking I'd given him and the compromising pictures I had had delivered to his wife and Baltimore's few remaining media outlets, but I still needed some serious help to get Lenny in the clear and nailing the Legg-Alexander kid.

To finally make things right, I needed someone on my side who was on the right side of the law—or at least whose business card said he was.

I hated asking people for favors, but this time I had to bite the bullet. After a quick shower and a couple of cups of black coffee, I had a plan, but to pull this off, I needed to dress the part.

I opened my closet and eyed the offerings. Since I rarely wore anything but jeans and sweats, it was slim pickings for any clothes other than those suitable for dog-walking or kickboxing. The few dresses and skirts hanging forlornly in my closet were hopelessly out of date. I rolled my eyes in disgust and closed the door.

I rummaged through my underwear drawer and pulled out on an old push-up bra I'd used for a long-ago Halloween costume. My breasts sat high and tight. Perfect.

In my bottom drawer, I located a red V-neck sweater that had shrunk in the wash and was now two sizes too small. I put it on and reached into my gym bag for my running tights. At least they made my butt look good. And I did have strong thighs from all those hours of roundhouse kicks to the heavy bag. I didn't have any high heels, so my motorcycle boots would have to do.

Next I tamed my hair with a big dollop of mousse. My bangs were now plastered against my forehead and the rest of my hair hung like wet sheets. Christ, I looked like Joan Jett's evil twin. I soldiered on. In the bottom of an old purse, I found some cracked make-up. I smeared some pink lipstick on my chapped lips and did the best I could with the caked mascara and blue eye shadow. I capped off the effect with some dangly earrings and a black ribbon around my neck.

I was ready. I pulled Officer Don Williams's card from the back pocket of my jeans and dialed. He picked up on the first ring.

"Williams," he said flatly.

"Hi, Don, it's Jane from the Hub Cap," I said, trying to sound sexy. "I just got up and was thinking about you. I believe you owe me something important."

"So, I was on your mind?" he said. Then his voice turned low and flirty. "What part of me was on your mind?"

Men were such idiots. It didn't take much to get their attention.

"I was hoping we could get some coffee," I purred. I knew he'd take the bait.

"I can do that. Just let me finish arresting and booking some bad guys and I'll meet you at Pete's Diner. Gimme 30 minutes."

Pete's Diner was a greasy spoon near the city jail and across the street from police headquarters. It was run by ex-cons hoping to stay clean. The food was inedible. The coffee was worse.

Pete's parking lot was filled with police cars. It figured that cops and criminals couldn't stay away from each other, even when they were both off-duty.

I checked my appearance in the rear-view mirror. I became self-conscious of my outfit. I was all dolled up, or at least I felt that way. I hadn't worn makeup in years and the push-up bra was cutting off the circulation to my lungs.

I felt vulnerable without my black leather jacket and jeans. Who was I trying to kid? I felt like an ugly duckling doing a poor imitation of a low-rent swan.

Still, if I was going to be able to carry out my plan, I had to be all the way in.

I walked into Pete's and slid into a booth. A loose spring poked my butt through the torn, red fake-leather seat. I started cracking my knuckles, but stopped when I saw Don walk in. He gave me a big, lopsided smile. "How you doing, little lady?" he said, tipping his hat. I smiled wanly.

Don sat next to me and immediately put his arm around me. Good—step one of my plan was working.

"Two coffees light and sweet," Don said to the waiter. The waiter took our order without making eye contact, then scurried away like a frightened mouse.

"I booked that guy last year for knocking over a convenience store in Glen Burnie," Don said in explanation. "He's not really a bad guy. Got a family and kids to support in Florida somewhere."

"Listen, Don," I said, leaning forward and pulling my sweater down an inch to show a little cleavage. "You seem like a decent guy. I need your help to put a real bad guy away." I reached into my purse and pulled out Lenny's pictures. I moved our stained coffee mugs out of way and cleared the greasy table.

"Remember that boy with the hole in his head in Mt. Jefferson? I know who killed him and where to find him."

I slapped the black-and-white pictures of Jared Legg-Alexander down in front of Don. "Here's your killer."

I jabbed my finger at the photo of Legg-Alexander grinning like a sick maniac. "His name is Jared Legg-Alexander and he's the freak son of some hot-shot lawyer in Mt. Jefferson. He killed that boy and now my cousin Lenny is being framed for the murder. You're the only person who can help me."

"Lenny Ronson's your cousin?" Don said. "I used to see him at all the crime scenes. He introduced me to my now-ex-wife. I was at a double homicide at Lexington Towers. Must have been around 1986. Lenny was taking pictures for the newspaper and he had this good-looking reporter with him. She was just out of Loyola College. Poor thing had never been south of Roland Park, much less seen a murder. She looked like she was going to faint."

He was smiling a little now.

"I took her to Pete's for burgers after we'd mopped up and we hit it off. We had a good couple of years together."

I didn't have time for this stuff.

"Don, are you gonna help Lenny or not?" I asked point-blank. I didn't want to hear any more about his ex-wife. I was already humiliated and exasperated enough.

"What did you say that kid's name was?"

"It's Jared Legg-Alexander. He and his high-rent corporate-lawyer father have fingered Lenny for killing that kid.

"Look at those pictures, Don. It's all there in black and white. Lenny saw the murder happening. He didn't kill the kid. He's a wimp. And he's terrified of cops, so he ran away. You've got the wrong person for this murder. The photos are your damn evidence."

Don was staring at my chest. His gaze was fixed on my boobs. I snapped my fingers in front of him to see if he'd snap out of it. He kept staring.

So I played my final card. "OK, I'll sleep with you if you help me get Lenny cleared of all these bullshit charges."

"Huh?" Don said, finally looking up at me. "You'll have sex with me?"

I was completely humiliated. I couldn't believe I'd sunk so low. I'd just propositioned a cop to save my cousin's ass, my underwear was giving me a wedgie and I had no more cards left to play. Then I threw my arms around him and started crying. It was all I had left.

The waiter slunk over the table and slipped the check under the napkin holder. Don put a $20 bill on the table.

"Bring me a box of tissues for the lady, Bubs," Don said as he held me. "And keep the change."

Don handed me his napkin. I blew my nose and starting blubbering all over his uniform. I felt like an emotional train wreck. I wondered if I was getting my period.

"Of course I'll help you," Don said gently. "You don't have to sleep with me to get me to do what's right. Contrary to what you might think, I'm a stand-up guy. Not all men are pigs. But just so you know, your boobs do look hot in that sweater."

Don took my hand and continued, "I know a judge who owes me a favor. I found his teenage son with a hooker in a motel on Pulaski Highway last month. The judge begged me to let the kid go with just a warning. I didn't want to do it, but I knew I'd catch hell from the sergeant if I booked the kid. I'll head over to the Mitchell Courthouse and talk to hizzoner. No one likes to avoid scandals more than judges."

"Thanks for your help, Don. I'm not usually like this, it's that ..."

I looked down and crossed my legs. Yup, my period had started.

"It's OK, Jane," Don said, holding my hand a little tighter. "I've gotta do the right thing here. We both do."

11 Jared Goes Down

What the hell was wrong with me? Wearing makeup. Kissing cops in diners. Sucking up to transvestite bail bondsmen. I didn't do things like this, at least not under normal circumstances. But my life had gotten so screwed up in the last 24 hours that I couldn't tell my elbow from my ass.

The only thing left to do was go home and take Archie out for a pee. I drove away from the Inner Harbor, past the Supermax prison, and inched my way in the choke-hold traffic onto the Jones Falls Expressway. "Christ, what a clown circus," I cursed. A rusted-out hoopdie and a neon-green Prius sandwiched me in the middle lane.

I lit another cigarette, hit the brakes and cut into the right lane. A chorus of horns sounded behind me. I floored my ancient Toyota, zoomed up the shoulder and exited onto Falls Road. It was barely 8 o'clock in the morning and already people were sitting on the stoops of their broken-down rowhouses, drinking beer and dragging on cigarettes.

I pulled up to a red light and saw a woman leaning against a telephone pole. Her face was a rictus of worry lines and wrinkles, and her dark blue sweatshirt and grimy jeans hung like droopy window shades on her emaciated frame. She could have been 30 or 60. She looked like life had beaten the crap out of her, then come back for another round.

The crone squinted hard at me while I waited for the light to turn. She held a cigarette in her boney claw as she walked to my car and rapped on my window. "Got a light, sister?" she said, her face inches from the glass. Against my better judgment, I cranked the window down halfway and offered her my Harley Davidson lighter. She fired up a Camel and took a heavy drag. We stared at each other like two dogs at a standoff. Just as the light turned green, she leaned in and gripped my edge of my window. Her gnarled fingers were stained yellow and her face was inches from mine. I smelled the stale beer on her breath.

"It ain't worth being a shit, kid. I can see it in your face—you're trying too hard to be a bitch. And that don't get you nowhere but some rat hole of a corner in Hampden looking like dog crap and feelin' a million times worse. I'm your cautionary tale. Now get the fuck out of here and don't ever come back this way."

I hit the gas pedal hard and flew up the road. I looked in my rearview mirror to make sure the harpie wasn't running after my car. It was like a zombie apocalypse.

I was still shaking when I pulled into my driveway. I fished the key out of my purse and jammed it into the door. Archie charged toward me, knocking me flat on my back. He planted his front legs on my boobs, lowered his head and started licking my face like it was a melting ice cream cone.

"Jesus Christ, Archie, you know about the 'no French kissing' rule!" I said, trying not to open my mouth wide enough for him to stick his spade-shaped tongue down my throat. I tucked and rolled to my right side and pushed the beast off me. Archie trotted after me as I walked into my bedroom. I stripped down to my underwear and splashed cold water on my face. Then I grabbed some clean jeans, a turtleneck sweater and a windbreaker.

"Archie, dog park! We're outta here," I snapped.

My skin started to crawl as we neared the dog park. I'd forgotten that there was a lacrosse tournament. SUVs and Hummers were jammed into the parking lot next to the dog park. I took off Archie's harness and let him run in between the cars. He immediately lifted his leg and let loose a powerful arc of piss onto a Chevy Blazer's front wheel. "Good boy, Archie," I beamed.

A car horn blasted me like a mortar shell exploding in my ear. I looked up to see Jared Legg-Alexander behind the wheel of a jet-black Land Rover, pulling up in front of me. Archie growled and bared his teeth as Jared and his mother climbed out of the car. Jared fixed me in a death stare, then winked maliciously. His mother tottered by on her inappropriate spiky heels, a hot-pink iPhone plastered to her ear.

"The head lacrosse scout from Tompkins is here to see Jared play," she cooed. "I'm so incredibly excited. You know how important it is for Jared to play for the right school. We can't have him going to a public university. OK, darling; I'll see you later for chocolatinis. Ciao."

Chocolatinis? I didn't know whether to laugh or retch.

Jared heaved his lacrosse gear over his brutish shoulders and turned to me. "Sorry to hear your cousin Lenny's been arrested again. Oh, well, gotta keep the neighborhood trash-free."

Archie lunged for Jared's thigh. Jared jumped back. "Too bad Lenny can't have your dog for a cellmate in jail," he hissed.

"Yeah, it's a damn shame they don't have lacrosse at Supermax," I snarled.

"Sweetie, we can't keep the Tompkins scout waiting," Jared's mother said. She picked up her oversized designer purse and tottered toward the field, her stiletto heels sinking into the turf.

My cellphone rang. It was Don. "Where are you? I've got an arrest warrant for Jared Legg-Alexander that I'm ready to execute."

I loved it when Don got all cop-talk with me.

"I'm at the dog park. Legg-Alexander and his mother are here. How'd you get the warrant so fast?"

"Judge Harris owed me a big favor. I told him if he didn't give me the arrest warrant, I was going to have to bust his kid for excessive stupidity with ugly hookers. Last time I checked that was still a crime— even in Baltimore. I'll be there in five minutes. Stand down, Jane. Don't do anything stupid."

I walked toward the crowd that had gathered to watch the lacrosse game. I kept my eye on the Legg-Alexanders. Jared's mother stood next to a guy in a blue-and-white Tompkins windbreaker. At least half of the crowd was wearing blue-and-white outfits with the Tompkins logo. Herd mentality, I thought. So much for any original thinking from this bunch of losers.

Jared loped onto the field and took off his shirt. I stood in back of his mother so I could monitor the situation. She was talking the coach's ear off about Jared being a lacrosse legacy since his father played for Tompkins.

I was bored stiff, so I only half-listened to Jared's mother as she rattled on about how she and her husband were board members of this and that foundation, and how much money they raised for charities.

I started thinking about the ass-kicking I'd delivered to Brice Legg-Alexander and his failed promise to use his connections to get Lenny out of jail. All the Legg-Alexanders were a piece of work.

I had a boatload of unfinished business with this family. All I needed was some more time to plan my revenge.

The Tompkins coach just kept nodding, barely listening. His gaze was fixed on Jared, who was showing off to the crowd by doing one-armed push-ups. Jared's teammates were running laps around the field or lobbing shots at the goalie. For the life of me, I couldn't fathom why Baltimore was infatuated with this idiotic sport.

The referee trotted onto the field to signal the end of the warm-up session. Just then, a police siren shrieked. People grabbed their folding chairs and jumped out of the way as Don floored his cruiser through the throng. His brakes screeched as he pulled up the edge of the lacrosse field and jumped out. Jared looked up from his push-ups. His teammates froze as Don strode toward him like the Terminator stalking John Connor.

Don was all business. He had his dark cop sunglasses on and his mouth was grimly set. His hand rested on his Glock.

Don was three feet away and closing rapidly when Jared bolted toward the woods. Don's reaction was faster than I thought possible for someone wearing 35 pounds of police gear. He sprinted down the field like he was going for an Olympic medal. Someone in crowd applauded. Jared looked over his shoulder as Don executed a flying tackle. Jared landed face down in the turf. Don squatted down and zip-cuffed Jared's arms behind his back.

"Jared Legg-Alexander, you have the right to remain silent ..." Don intoned to the back of Jared's head. A collective gasp arose from the lacrosse field. More people applauded. Out of the corner of my eye, I saw Jared's mother walking awkwardly toward her son. A yard before she got to him, her high-heeled shoes lodged in the grass and she tumbled end over end before landing in front of a group of snickering children.

Don dragged Jared to his feet. Jared was almost a half-foot taller than Don, but his head was bowed and his shaggy hair hung over his face in a corona of shame. His shoulders heaved and he started crying. Someone lobbed a bottle of Gatorade that hit Jared squarely on his head. "Mom .... Mom ... help me!" he wailed to his mother.

"Stop bawling, you big pussy," Don barked as he frog-marched Jared through the crowd. A dark stain spread over Jared's shorts. He must have shit himself. For a second I almost felt sorry for him.

Don shoved Jared into the back of his police cruiser and slammed the door. Then he turned toward the crowd and smiled.

The crowd came to life. As if on cue, everyone pulled out cellphones, iPhones and Blackberries, and started texting. A knot of kids began taking videos of Jared crying in the back seat of the police car. One cheeky brat gave Jared the finger, then spat on the window.

Jared's mother sat on the field with a blank expression on her face. The Tompkins lacrosse coach rolled his eyes at her and grimaced. Guess he'll have to find another criminal to recruit, I thought.

I walked toward the police car. Jared was in custody, but I wasn't happy. I had a bad feeling that this nightmare wasn't over yet. Too many questions were still unanswered. Would Don's connection to the judge keep Lenny out of jail for good? Would Jared be charged with murder, and would that charge stick?

I was sure that Jared's dad still had some dirty tricks up his sleeve. I might have won the first round, but this game was far from over.

People like Jared Legg-Alexander did not get charged with murder. They bought their way out of trouble and let everyone else deal with the consequences.

In all likelihood, Jared would probably spend a few hours behind bars, but would sleep in his own bed tonight. His parents were loaded and knew people in even higher places who would get Jared off with probation and some bullshit community service.

And the dead boy from other side of Northern Parkway? He'd end up just as another crime statistic in a city that already had too many murdered men, women and children. His death would be lucky to merit a two-sentence mention in the *Baltimore Sun*. Meanwhile, the boy's family would mourn him for the rest of their lives. There's justice in Baltimore for you: deaf, dumb and blind.

Where the hell was Archie? He wasn't at my side anymore. "Archie, you S.O.B., get over here," I yelled. I heard a bark. I looked over at the police cruiser and saw Archie leaning out of the front passenger window.

"There you are, you blockhead," I said as I jogged over and patted his head.

Don held the door open for me and I slid into the passenger side next to Archie. Archie licked my face, then began licking his balls. Same old same old.

I tapped the safety glass separating me from Jared to get his attention. Jared looked up with a withered expression. I flipped him the double bird and turned to Don. I wanted to kiss him, but not in front of Legg-Alexander.

"I got your bad guy for you, Jane, just like I promised," Don said, smiling like a million dollars. "Judge Harris hates pretty boys who play lacrosse, especially when their fathers make big campaign donations to his opponents in an election year."

"You'd better be right about that," I said. "I'm not going through this bullshit again to get Lenny out of jail. And, hey—speaking of that jailbird, where the hell is he?"

Don started up the car and eased it out of the parking lot. "Don't worry, Lenny and the gang are waiting for us at the Hub Cap with some cold ones on the house. You've become a local hero to those guys. Bad girl nails bad guy. As we say around the station house, you're good police, Jane. Jared Legg-Alexander went down thanks to you. We'll head over to the Hub Cap after I make a little detour to central booking to lock up pretty-boy Jared."

"Don, I ...," I began. "I really appreciate everything you've ..."

"Oh, hell, Jane, don't get sentimental on me," he said, squeezing my thigh. "Tonight, the wings are on me."

About the author

Jill Yesko's 20⁺-year writing career includes stints as a reporter and a contributing writer to publications from *Fitness Swimmer* to *Escape* magazine. Along the way, she has written about everything from hiking the mud flats of northern Holland to body piercing. After taking a solo trip around the world, Jill was profiled as an "adventurous traveler" in *O, The Oprah Magazine*.

Before entering the field of journalism, Jill was a national-class cyclist and graduate student in geography. A New Jersey native, Jill now lives in Baltimore and patrols the local dog parks with her basset hound. *Murder in the Dog Park* is her first novel.

Visit Jill at http://murderinthedogpark.blogspot.com.

Photo © Beau Monde Press 2012

CPSIA information can be obtained at www.ICGtesting.com
Printed in the USA
BVOW080707120712

294862BV00005B/1/P

9 780985 485207